Elizabeth must make a choice.

She continued searching the crowd, but her eyes were drawn back to the tall man. He turned his head and suddenly looked toward her. For one moment she thought that mentioning John Martin to someone for the first time in months was causing her to conjure him up. His gaze swept over her, and then suddenly he started. His eyes widened in unbelief.

Their eyes clung.

She stood motionless, hardly daring to breathe. Then she saw him straighten his shoulders. He started pushing through the crowd toward her.

"Why, I do declare, isn't that Mr. Hardy over there?" Mrs. Richmond panted beside her.

Elizabeth hardly heard her. That other familiar face loomed ever closer. Then he was in front of her. She was vaguely aware that Mrs. Richmond gave a startled gasp of recognition, but not once did she stop staring into John's blue eyes until he executed a very gentlemanly bow. But he said not a word. He just stood there waiting for her to either turn away or acknowledge him.

MARY HAWKINS has thoroughly enjoyed the ups and downs of thirty-four years of being a minister's wife at churches in various cities in New South Wales and Queensland, Australia. She and husband Ray have two married sons and one daughter, and are still waiting to be grandparents. Mary has long had a dream to write an historical series. "The Great Southland" series is the combination of her dream with details from family history. For Mary, the wonder of readers enjoying her writing efforts is a constant source of praise to the Lord Jesus she loves.

Books by Mary Hawkins

HEARTSONG PRESENTS
HP42—Search for Tomorrow
HP101—Damaged Dreams
HP129—Search for Yesterday
HP202—Search for Today

Don't miss out on any of our super romances. Write to us at the following address for information on our newest releases and club information.

Heartsong Presents Readers' Service
PO Box 719
Uhrichsville, OH 44683

Faith
in the Great Southland

Mary Hawkins

Heartsong Presents

For my dear sister, Shirley Rylance, who over the years has shared my love for books, as well as history—and above all, the love of Christ.

A note from the authors:
I love to hear from my readers! You may correspond with me by writing:
Mary Hawkins
Author Relations
PO Box 719
Uhrichsville, OH 44683

ISBN 1-57748-530-0

FAITH IN THE GREAT SOUTHLAND

All Scripture quotations are from the Authorized King James Version of the Bible unless otherwise noted.

All of the characters and events in this book are fictitious. Any resemblance to actual persons, living or dead, or to actual events is purely coincidental.

Cover illustration by Dominick Saponaro.

PRINTED IN THE U.S.A.

prologue

England, April 1835

The excited shouts of the crowd squeezed into the public gallery died away. A stillness descended on the courtroom as the judge impressively drew his gown around him at last and rapped his gavel again and again. He looked down at the papers on his desk briefly before staring again at the white-faced young man standing in the dock.

"John Martin, you have just been found guilty of the felonious slaying of Lord Farnley's gamekeeper, Jock Macallister."

A murmur swept through the people. The heavily veiled woman at the farthest corner of the room unsuccessfully tried to stifle a desperate sob. A few heads of the curious swung toward her. She shrank back on her hard wooden bench, one dainty, black-gloved hand pressing the veil to her lips. They stared, but then Judge Wedgewood's ponderous tones brought every eye back to him.

"Do you have anything to say before I pronounce your sentence?"

Every head swung to the condemned man. His tall, strong figure stiffened. He raised his head even higher. As they had many times during his trial, his dark eyes desperately searched the room.

"As God is my witness, I declare once more that I am not guilty!" His slightly accented voice rang with desperate conviction. "The guilty person knows this, and one day. . ." His voice choked with rage and despair. "One day he will have to face an eternal Judge greater than you, your honor."

An angry murmur swept through the people at the fellow's effrontery.

The judge adjusted his wig, picked up his gavel, and

brought it crashing down in front of him. He stared back at the man before him from beneath his beetling eyebrows and waited until all was dead quiet again.

"Indeed, young man," he replied at last in his impressive tones, "that will be *all* our lot one day."

Judge Wedgewood picked up the pile of papers before him and shuffled them neatly together. When he had laid them down carefully he raised his head and said angrily, "I find that you are an arrogant liar who, in a final act of desperation to try and escape conviction for your dastardly crime, dared to declare himself to be the son and heir of my old friend, Lord Farnley."

"I am his son!"

Angry shouts erupted from the crowd. "There's no way old righteous 'Arry would ever 'ave a Frenchy foreigner for a son," someone shouted.

A discreetly clad gentleman in dark clothes bowed his head to hide a delighted smile as Judge Wedgewood banged his gavel until order was restored once again.

The prisoner only glared at the spectator for a moment. Several times already had he protested his mother was Spanish, not French.

"Lord Farnley could not be here in person to refute your preposterous claim because of the desperate illness of his dear wife, but unfortunately for you he has sent the court a sworn statement that you are nothing more than a stranger he kindly took into his employ some months ago."

The prisoner stared back at him defiantly for a moment, but then his shoulders drooped in sudden defeat.

Satisfied, the judge paused and drew something black from the receptacle buried deep in his robes. A hushed murmur raced through the crowd. It was the black cap.

"Prisoner at the bar! Have you anything to urge why sentence of death should not be passed upon you?"

John Martin raised his head and looked steadily at the judge. Then his gaze again swept the room. It caught and held the pale eyes of the gentleman in the front row. The gentleman's eyes dropped first.

The slightest frown twitched the prisoner's ash-white face. Then he suddenly straightened his shoulders and stood to his full height as he turned calmly to the judge.

"I have said all I can, your honor, except to declare once again my complete innocence and pray that one day the guilty man will be found."

The experienced judge stared back intently for a long moment as though impressed despite himself. "It is in my power to sentence you to hang by the neck until you are dead for such a heinous crime."

The man before him did not flinch. This he had known throughout the trial.

"Oh, no, no. Not that!" a woman's despairing voice cried out.

John Martin's head swung sharply around, searching the crowd eagerly.

The gavel thundered again.

"Instead, I will have mercy on you. John Martin, I sentence you to be transported to the great Southland of Australia for the term of your natural life!"

And we know that all things work together for good to them that love God, to them who are called according to his purpose.
Romans 8:28

one

September 1835

The large traveling coach lurched on the uneven surface as it turned and slowly approached the wharf. Elizabeth Waverley leaned eagerly out the window for her first glimpse of the ship that would eventually reunite her with her father.

"For goodness sake child, do show some decorum," wailed the stout woman beside her as she pressed a handkerchief daintily to her nose. "And how you can be so pleased to leave me so suddenly like this after all I've done for you I'll never know. You know Lord Weldon's son was on the verge of proposing."

"Oh, Aunt Sophia," Elizabeth began impatiently as she subsided. Then she paused, swallowing back for the hundredth time all she would like to have told her aunt and chaperone about the highly esteemed Frederick Weldon and his sly ways. After holding her tongue for so long about their last encounter, now was not the time to upset her dear aunt any more.

She glanced at the other wide-eyed occupant of the carriage and then shrugged. In the close confines of the ship, poor, frightened Betsy, whom her uncle had somehow persuaded to be her maid for the next few months, would undoubtedly get to know most of her business—already did in the way servants always seemed to.

More gently she said to her aunt, "There has never been the least chance I would ever marry anyone here so far from home. Dear Aunt, you know I always intended to return to Australia as soon as Father would let me."

Sophia Lantry straightened. "But that's just it, child. He

hasn't asked for your return. Couldn't you at least have waited until you heard from him?"

"No, I finished at St. Peter's Lady's Academy last year. As far as I'm concerned, my education was the only reason I let him persuade me to come to England."

Elizabeth's voice had remained quiet, but her aunt had heard that implacable note in her voice too many times over the last three years to do more than sigh and say peevishly, "Well, after all I've done for you, the least you could do is show some sorrow at saying good-bye so suddenly to us all."

The older woman was suddenly enveloped in strong young arms and kissed soundly. "Oh, Aunt, you know I'm sad at leaving you and Uncle Harry and all the friends I've made here. It's just. . .just. . .with Father's old friends returning on this ship it was just too good an opportunity to miss."

Sophia returned her embrace and then pushed her away. "Oh, I know, Elizabeth, I know." She sighed again. "I should, you've told me enough over the years. You were born in New South Wales, that dreadful place is your home, and despite all the attractions of England you've been homesick for the smell of eucalyptus ever since you got here—or some such nonsense."

Elizabeth's laugh rang out. "And for the freedom of the open spaces. And it's not a dreadful place," she protested vigorously. "It has the most beautiful harbor, wonderful beaches, and the wildlife—" She stopped abruptly and laughed softly at her aunt's genteel snort before once again turning eagerly to the window as the coach came slowly to a halt.

In a few moments the two women had descended with the help of her aunt's groom. They stared around at all the hustle and bustle of a busy wharf just prior to a ship leaving port. Miss Betsy Bent stumbled slowly out behind them to gaze in fascination at the tall masted ship at the center of furious activity.

"Elizabeth!"

The absolute horror in her aunt's voice made Elizabeth catch her bottom lip firmly with her teeth. When her aunt had insisted on accompanying her to the *Royal Lady* in place of her uncle, who had succumbed to a severe episode of gout, she had hoped fervently that the other "passengers" would have been on board the ship and out of sight by the time they arrived.

Now the moment of truth had come, and she braced herself, knowing that her aunt had also seen the long line of poor wretches in drab gray prison clothes stumbling up the gang-plank onto the ship.

Before she could respond, her aunt cried out, "Elizabeth, oh, my dear girl, it's a convict transport ship! You can't go all that way with criminals on board!"

Betsy Bent suddenly wailed in a shrill voice, "Convicts! Criminals. . .no, no! Madam. . .I can't go. No matter what the master says I won't go!" With that she burst into tears and climbed back into the coach, slamming the door firmly behind her.

Aunt Sophia wrung her hands, looked at Elizabeth's face, and then went back to the coach to beg the servant not to fail them.

Elizabeth was silent. When Dr. Richmond had warned her he was traveling back as the surgeon on board a transport ves-sel, she had only hesitated for a moment and then insisted that made no difference to her.

Her father had endured this journey as a convict more than forty years ago. It was something the now wealthy Australian pastoralist never talked about. Oh, over the years she had pieced together some of the torture he had endured on that voyage, but something deep inside her had made her want to understand more about the hard, solitary man who was her father.

Aunt Sophia grabbed her arm and actually shook it. "I can't talk any sense into that stupid woman. Elizabeth, you can't possibly go on that ship, especially not without a maid!"

Elizabeth opened her mouth to respond, to tell her she would share Mrs. Richmond's maid or do for herself, but nothing was going to stop her from going on this ship. Before she could utter a word, a loud commotion made them both swing around.

A small detachment of mounted soldiers approached. In their wake came a large coach. As it lumbered to a stop not far from them, the horsemen immediately surrounded the vehicle in a wide circle, noisily forcing back the crowd of curious people.

There was a chill wind blowing off the water, but the men crammed miserably together on the top of the coach had not a coat or blanket between them. All was confusion, noise and dust for a few moments. Several loud orders were shouted, and the men stood. A few clutched their miserable bundles and began to scramble to the ground. They weren't moving fast enough, and some were seized and dragged roughly down by their guards to sprawl in the dirt.

Simultaneously the doors of the coach were swung open and other men stumbled their way out to stand shivering on the wharf. The poor wretches' movements were accompanied by the rattle and clash of metal on metal, and Elizabeth drew in a quick breath. However, she quickly noticed that unlike the long line of other convicts already boarding the ship, at least these poor creatures wore individual fetters on their hands and feet.

An officer approached rapidly from the ship, calling out, "This the consignment from York?"

Her gaze still riveted on the group of prisoners, Elizabeth heard a harsh voice respond, "Aye, and a long, hard journey it's been."

"Elizabeth, you can't go on that ship with those dreadful men!"

At her aunt's loud, now almost hysterical cry, Elizabeth saw one of the prisoners, an erect man who stood head and shoulders taller than those around him, swing his head toward them. For one long, piercing moment, dark eyes from beneath thick, black eyebrows swept over her tall figure from her red-gold curls peeping out around the hood of her traveling cloak to her sensibly shod feet.

Then his eyes met hers. For one piercing moment he studied her intently as though committing her face to memory.

Then he scowled before turning sharply away and shuffling forward toward the ship.

Elizabeth shivered. Hardly hearing her aunt's continuing protests, she stared after the convict. Despite not being able to take more than a small step because of his chains, he carried himself erectly. His clothes might be as filthy as the others, but they had once been of good cut and quality.

For one brief moment there had been eager anticipation in the dark gaze. Then there had been only the deepest anger, even hatred. As he had swung away, his shoulders stiff and unyielding, some other expression had touched his face, something that could have been utter despair.

❧

A woman called Elizabeth. How ironic.

For one brief, insane moment, John Martin had wondered if Beth Farnley had come at last to insist he was innocent, to stop this madness that had left him rotting in prison all those dreary winter months since his arrest and mockery of a trial. He was sure it had been her voice that day. . .

"Move along there!"

The hard prod in his back forced John to stumble against the short, thin man in front of him. That poor man had unwittingly fallen foul of the guards on the long journey to London and was in much heavier chains than the rest of them. He almost fell, but John managed to grab him and pull him upright. Blank, empty eyes turned toward him.

"Sorry," John muttered.

It cost him another blow to his back. "No talking, there! Come on, you scum, the sooner you're on board the sooner you'll all be snug."

As the harsh, sarcastic voice cursed them, frozen limbs made them slip and stumble toward the long gangway. Someone behind John cried out in pain.

Then a boy's voice rang out. "Father, where's my father?"

The man in front of John swung around again. His eyes flared to life. "Tim!" he cried in a great shout. "Here, son, I'm here!"

His last words were drowned out by the shouting of the guards as they tried to stop the darting, twisting figure rushing toward the convicts.

The boy was close. He never took his eyes off the man in front of John. Then, as the boy's father gave a desperate shout of warning, John too saw the danger. In trying to dodge a burly soldier, the child had moved too close to the edge of the wharf. He stumbled, tried to gain his balance, and then disappeared. Seconds later, they heard the splash of water.

For a fraction of a second Tim's father froze, then with a loud wail, the man stumbled forward. With horror John knew he was about to follow his son into the cold, dark water. Neither father nor son would have a chance. Those heavy iron fetters would drag them down.

John grabbed the man as he tried to push his way past him. "I'll get him, you fool," he muttered, and despite the sudden uproar of the crowd and the shouted orders of the guards, he dived into the dark water.

Almost as soon as he could walk, John had learned how to swim in the river on his grandfather's property in Spain. Normally it would have been no great task to scoop the dazed boy out of the freezing water, but the light chains on his own arms and legs pulled him down.

Months of prison food and lack of exercise had weakened him more than he had realized. It took every ounce of energy he could muster to grab the dazed, floundering boy, cling to him with one hand, and hang on to a moss-covered pier with the other to prevent them both from slipping back under the black, filthy water. It seemed forever before rough hands hauled them out. John collapsed in a heap onto the wharf.

As he lay gasping for breath, he was vaguely conscious of a loud woman's voice in the crowd above them demanding to be let through. A rustle of petticoats drew closer. A gentle hand was using a delicate, perfumed handkerchief to wipe away some of the debris and slime that clung to his face.

He opened his eyes and stared directly into the greenest

eyes he had ever seen.

"Are you all right, sir?"

Her cultured voice was soft, like the whisper of a breeze through the fields of corn in the paddocks at home. Her hood had been thrust back. Those red-gold curls had escaped the ribbons tying them back from her beautiful face. They tumbled in glorious profusion to her shoulders.

She was staring at him anxiously as though she really cared that he should have come to no harm.

And she had called him "sir."

That first gentle courtesy he had received since he had been arrested in a Yorkshire wood, was worth a dunking in the foul, freezing Thames.

"I'll be fine, and. . .and thank you, madam."

For a timeless moment after his breathless whisper, their eyes locked. His hand moved instinctively up toward her face. The irresistible velvet texture of her glowing skin felt as soft as it looked. Suddenly a soldier thrust her aside. Even so, something deep inside him suddenly exulted. She had made no attempt to flinch away from the touch of his large, wet hand.

"That'll be all, madam," the harsh voice of the officer in charge ordered. "We'll get him on board with the others now."

Rough hands hauled John to his feet and shoved him forward. He heard the woman called Elizabeth give a sharp protest, but then he was stumbling up the gangplank, even colder now in his soaking wet clothes. Despair once again settled over him like a cloak as he at last descended into the dark hold of the ship and away from the goodness and sweetness of her face.

⁂

Elizabeth stood frozen to the spot, watching as the man was half dragged, half pushed up the gangplank to at last disappear after his fellow convicts.

Then one gloved hand crept to the cheek he had touched. . . had touched almost reverently. That desperate, hungry look in his eyes. . .eyes that weren't brown after all, but the darkest blue.

"Oh, Tim, Tim, you foolish boy! I told you and told you they'd never let you near him."

"But I prayed so hard, Ma!"

The weary hopelessness in the woman's low voice and the boy's sad cry captured Elizabeth's attention. She swung around to see a neatly clad young woman a few years older than herself bending over the shivering, wet boy.

Elizabeth ignored her aunt's even louder gasp of horrified protest and crouched down beside them, relieved to see the sobbing boy seemed little worse for his dunking.

She straightened and said briskly to the gaping groom, "The child's freezing. Quickly, that rug from the carriage."

The convict must be even colder in his wet clothes. She forced her thoughts away from him to concentrate on the boy whose life he had saved. Taking the rug from the groom, she wrapped the boy carefully in its warmth.

His mother put her arms around him tightly and said in a shaking voice, "Thank you, Miss."

Elizabeth hesitated and then asked softly, "Your husband is being transported to Australia?"

Pain-filled eyes looked at her. "Ten years they're sending him away for. Ten years! All because he was foolish enough to get involved with some political agitators trying to make a better life for me and his family. He's a good man, not. . .not a criminal! I've been trying and trying to get someone to listen to me, to even let me and the boys go to New South Wales to be near him. Otherwise. . ."

Her voice broke, and tears began rolling down her cheeks. She looked toward the ship. "I don't know if my Timothy will survive ten years out there." Her voice dropped to a choked whisper. "We'll never see him again."

Had this been what it had been like for her father's family?

Elizabeth doubted it. Instead of coming from such an obviously educated and no doubt respectable background as this woman did, her father had been spawned in the black slums of London, not knowing anything but a life of misery and despair, trying to survive by petty thieving until fate in the guise of a harsh magistrate had sent him to the then new penal colony far across the seas.

"Things. . .things aren't as bad for the convicts now as they were years ago, especially if he doesn't re-offend," Elizabeth said softly.

The woman straightened and studied Elizabeth for a moment. A bitter light filled her eyes. "Not as bad? Did you see how thin he was, how cold? Why there wasn't a coat amongst the lot of them, and I even sent a special warm one to the prison for him. Goodness knows what happened to it— probably on the back of some guard who thought it too good for a convict to own!" She shuddered. "And those horrible chains. . ."

Elizabeth's aunt pulled at her arm. "Elizabeth, we have to talk while there's still time to change your mind about going on this ship!"

The woman's eyes widened. "You're going on the ship?" she asked eagerly. "All the way to Australia?"

Elizabeth nodded briefly, resisting the insistent tug on her arm. "What is your husband's name?"

"Timothy Hardy." She drew in a quick breath. "If. . .if you could see your way clear to find out how he goes, and even. . . perhaps. . ."

Elizabeth turned to her aunt and said firmly, "Why don't you start up the gangway, Aunt Sophia. I'll only be a moment more."

Aunt Sophia searched her charge's eyes for a long moment and then shrugged resignedly. "I do hope your boy is no worse for his accident, Mrs. Hardy," she said stiffly before nodding to her and moving away.

Elizabeth scrabbled for writing materials in her large reticule. "Perhaps I could send a note to you about the voyage, Mrs. Hardy," she offered gently and was amply rewarded by the look of profound gratitude in the mother's and son's faces as she carefully wrote down their address.

Elizabeth smiled, said her farewells, and went to follow her aunt. Then she paused. "I don't suppose by any chance you know the name of the man who rescued your son?" she asked hesitantly.

"While. . .while he was making me hang on to him, he told me his name was John," the small boy said in a choked voice. "He. . .he said not to fret—he'd look out for my father."

"John!" exclaimed his mother. "I wonder if that's the John Martin my Timothy mentioned in his letter telling me when they were sailing. Why, he's a murderer, just escaped hanging he did. Transported for life instead."

Elizabeth was motionless for a moment. Suddenly a vivid picture of angry, hatred-filled eyes transformed to a wondering, bemused gaze searching out her very soul.

"He was still a very brave man," she said quietly, and then impulsively kissed the tearful Mrs. Hardy before smiling gently and turning away toward the ship.

She reached the bottom of the gangplank and paused. Closing her eyes, she whispered under her breath, "Oh, God, keep us all safe. Watch over those poor men and give me ever Your strength and compassion to do what is right. And. . .and comfort John Martin and. . .and bring him faith and. . .and. . ."

Her eyes flew open. Now, where had that thought come from? She had nearly added the words "someone to love him."

Taking a deep breath, she straightened and continued forward into the ship that would be her home for the next few months.

two

"All settled in, Elizabeth?"

"As best I can, I guess, Dr. Richmond." Elizabeth surveyed her tiny cabin a little ruefully and then smiled at the gray-haired man in its doorway. "It's even smaller than the one three years ago."

He smiled back sympathetically, and then he frowned slightly. "I am so dreadfully sorry that neither you nor my wife have a woman to wait on you."

Elizabeth chuckled. "But neither of us could know the other's maid would let her down. At least Mrs. Richmond's had the excuse of a sudden illness, whereas mine. . ." She grimaced.

"That may be so," he said severely, "but you would certainly have been more comfortable with help, and certainly more comfortable on pretty well any other ship except one specially fitted out to hold as much human cargo as possible." He hesitated and then added dryly, "I gained the impression that your esteemed aunt was unaware this was a transport vessel?"

As Aunt Sophia had been very vocal about that fact during her brief time on board before they had sailed, Elizabeth's eyes twinkled at him. "I'm only glad Mrs. Richmond was kind enough not to mention the fact we would be the only two women on board. Somehow there never seemed to be a right time to actually inform my aunt of what type of cargo was on this ship once she decided early this morning she had to say her farewells from the wharf."

He smiled a little reluctantly back at her. "Well, I'm sure the cabin boy will do all he can so you don't miss your maid too much, and perhaps later on we may find a suitable convict

18

to help." He paused and then added slowly, "It isn't going to be an easy voyage, Elizabeth."

She sobered immediately. "I know." She hesitated and then asked slowly, "Did you find out if that convict who rescued the boy is all right?"

He frowned. "He was still freezing cold in his wet clothes. I found him as soon as I could after we left the wharf and insisted he be given a change of clothes. But it'll be a miracle if he doesn't get at least a cold or sore throat for his efforts."

A few days later the surgeon was proved sadly right.

For security reasons the convicts were kept chained and locked below deck until the ship had been at sea several days. Elizabeth was one of the few people who did not suffer from the heaving of the ocean, but she felt deeply for those like the doctor's wife who were prostrated within hours of the ship reaching open sea. Several of the soldiers had also succumbed, but the ones she felt the most for were the wretched convicts below the hatches where she knew the ventilation was very poor.

Dr. Richmond had been kept extremely busy trying to help those afflicted with seasickness, and she saw little of him. Then one morning he knocked on her cabin door. She was shocked at his weary, drawn face.

"Oh, my dear sir, you look exhausted! Do come in."

He shook his head. "No time, my dear," he said abruptly. "I'm afraid I have to take you up on the offers of help for others besides my wife that you've persisted in making, Elizabeth."

"Of course, I'd be only too happy, but what about your poor wife?" Elizabeth asked anxiously. "I visited her before breakfast, and she told me all she wanted to do was sleep."

"Yes, yes, she's improving every hour. It's one of the convicts, that man John Martin you've asked after several times. I've been up with him all night trying to get his fever down. I'm afraid he developed a chill which went to his lungs. Now he's very ill."

The memory of those anguish-filled eyes had haunted Elizabeth, and she gave a distressed cry. Suddenly the doctor swayed. She grabbed his arm and pushed him onto a chair.

"I have wished all along you'd let me help others besides Mrs. Richmond," she exclaimed. "You've worn yourself out." She hesitated and then asked swiftly, dread filling her. "Is. . . is Mr. Martin going to die?"

"Not if I can help it," Dr. Richmond said grimly. "He's earned my utmost esteem for his assistance the last few days. Why, he's cleaned up and ministered to those poor wretches without a murmur of complaint, as tender as any woman could have—and most of them only cursed him for his efforts. And he hadn't been well himself—had a bit of a cough ever since his swim."

He sighed and continued wearily. "I should have kept a closer eye on him, I'm afraid, but that storm a couple nights ago caused havoc among the crew as well as the soldiers. Not until he went down like a log did I realize how ill he was. I've been up with him most of the night, but this morning his lungs are very congested, and he's delirious with a very high fever."

Elizabeth straightened. "You should be in bed yourself, Dr. Richmond," she said firmly. "As you may remember, I helped look after my mother before she died. Just tell me what you want me to do."

The doctor smiled slightly and murmured, "I remember very well. You were so young, but. . ."

He stopped abruptly, and she flushed and looked away from the admiration in his tired eyes.

"I've insisted the captain have our patient removed to a small cabin next to mine so you do not have to go below to the convict quarters," the doctor said briskly. "One of the cabin boys will assist you. I'll be there when I can, but as though I didn't have enough to do, two of the sailors managed to get into a fight last night. One has a cut that requires stitching."

He hesitated, and then said gruffly, "I then have to attend a flogging. The captain has ordered each man to have twenty lashes. You might like to avoid the deck later today."

There was silence for a long moment. "I've seen a man flogged once before, Dr. Richmond," Elizabeth said softly at last. "It was many more than twenty strokes, but it was not an experience I have ever wished to repeat."

Dr. Richmond frowned at her. "My dear young lady, whoever allowed you near such a thing? Surely your father. . ."

Elizabeth grimaced at his sudden discomfort. "No one. I slipped away from my father on a trip to Sydney. He was very angry with me," she added sadly.

And that was an understatement. Her father had been white-faced and more furious than she had ever seen him in all of her sixteen years.

She had often wondered if her rebellion that day had been the last straw for him and the reason he had made all the arrangements for her to go to England without even telling her. It had been only six months later that they had again made the long trip across the plains of western New South Wales and then over the Blue Mountains to Sydney for her to board the ship for the long sea voyage to England and the exclusive academy.

Well, that was all now thankfully behind her. She was on her way home at last, and she refused to think of her father's anger with her for not obtaining his permission for her to return. Instead, she would concentrate on doing all she could for the convict who had been in her thoughts constantly since she'd waved a slightly tearful farewell to Aunt Sophia and thankfully watched the shores of England recede into the distance.

❧

John felt as though he was floating in a burning sea. Then vaguely he realized he was being carried somewhere. Something banged painfully against his side. A rough voice began cursing and then stopped in midstream. A woman's sharp voice told someone to be more careful, then he slipped back again into that welcome land of darkness.

When he surfaced again, all he could hear was that sharp

voice again. It was inclined to fade in and out, but he thought it was saying something about removing those chains.

"Very good idea," he heard a strange voice croak.

There was a faint rustling, and then he smelled perfume. Forcing his eyes open, he saw an angel bending over him. Or was it? Were angels' eyes such a glorious green? Certainly no angel's eyes should be filled with such worry.

"Oh, sir, you are awake. How do you feel?"

The voice was no longer sharp but filled with tenderness. . . compassion. . .for him? Yes, only an angel would. . .

He opened his mouth and heard that strange voice croak again. "Green. . .thought. . .would be. . ." Then it was all too much effort, and he closed his eyes again and drifted back into that gray world waiting for him.

※

"The convicts are still far too restless to have their chains removed. Furthermore, Captain Longman agrees with me, Miss Waverley. He claims it's not worth the safety of all on board his ship."

Elizabeth forced back the furious words she longed to fling at this pompous officer. She glanced anxiously at the convict lying motionless on the narrow bunk. His eyes were closed again, and his face had a waxen hue that worried her immensely.

Drawing a deep breath, she said quietly, "I have been told that the usual practice is, or used to be, that all the chains are struck off once the ship is in blue water."

She did not consider it necessary to tell him that an old friend of her father, also an ex-convict, had told her this years before when she had tried to find out all she could about the treatment of the convicts, trying to fathom what had made her father the stern man he was.

Instead she added angrily, "But I repeat, I am not asking for the chains of all the convicts to be removed, just those of this unfortunate man whom I am convinced is far too ill to be of danger to anyone."

Lieutenant Edwards stared doubtfully down once again at the

large body on the narrow bunk. Elizabeth followed his gaze.

John Martin stirred, tossing his head from side to side for a moment, and then was still again. His hands moved restlessly, and the chains between his wrists tinkled slightly. Elizabeth forced herself not to wince as she had each time her attention had been drawn to the metal bands on his arms and ankles, especially the bruises and cuts caused by the irons.

"Look, Lieutenant, Dr. Richmond left me with express instructions. This man must be sitting propped up at all times, and he has to be rolled from side to side regularly as his body is sponged down to try and keep his fever controlled. His fetters make this extremely difficult, and they have actually hurt my arm. Look here, sir."

Elizabeth thrust the long sleeve on her dress back from her arm. Her forearm certainly did have a red mark on it, but it had not been caused when her patient had moved unexpectedly. Instead she had almost lost her balance from a roll of the ship and bumped into the iron on his leg. Her statement wasn't really an untruth. The patient had certainly nearly hit her a few times when he had thrashed around in his delirium.

The lieutenant had been looking at her arm intently—a little too intently, she suddenly realized. She did not at all like the sudden gleam in the slim young man's eyes.

Hastily she pulled the sleeve down and glanced around the cabin. "And where is that cabin boy I was promised would be helping me?"

The smirk disappeared. He scowled and said haughtily, "Still being sick like the rest of them, I should imagine, Miss Waverley."

Elizabeth had already discovered that she would need help with John Martin to get even a few sips of water past the dry, cracked lips when he was very restless. He was such a large man that she most certainly needed help to move him. In his delirium he had resisted her so much that she had indeed been afraid of being harmed by his chains, so instead she had commenced sponging his hot face and arms.

Then Lieutenant Edwards had burst into the cabin without so much as a tap on the door. The scowl on his face had made it obvious that the removal of one of his charges to this small but clean and tidy cabin had been against his will.

"Unfortunately, Mrs. Richmond is still not well enough herself to help me." Elizabeth chewed her top lip for a moment. Then she opened her eyes wide and smiled appealingly at the soldier. "Sir, I've been wondering if perhaps one of the other convicts might help me for a while. As you're probably aware, the whole ship's crew has to be on deck this afternoon for. . .for the punishment session."

The man's scowl deepened. She conjured up the sweetest smile she could and was rewarded by the slightly dazed look that replaced the scowl.

"I really do need help, sir," she pleaded prettily. "Dr. Richmond has been so good to me, letting me travel under his and his wife's chaperonage, and I do want to look after this patient of his the very best I can. The poor man's already worn himself out looking after us all during these rough seas."

She was rewarded by the softening of the lieutenant's face and the smile that tilted his slightly too full lips. One long finger tapped on his chin. Her patient moved restlessly again, and she was glad of the excuse to break eye contact as she hastened to try to restrain his arms as they again moved jerkily.

This time the chain lying across his chest did fly against her hand. Her hand stung only slightly, but it was too good an opportunity to miss. She gave a little scream and let the tears that had been threatening ever since she had seen the bruised and bloodied wrists and ankles flood her eyes. She turned beseechingly toward the hapless Lieutenant Edwards.

He immediately sprang to her assistance and tried to restrain the man he was ultimately responsible for. "I. . .I see that you do indeed need help, Miss Waverley," he said reluctantly at last, "but I'm not sure if there's a decent enough man among the convicts I'd trust to assist you."

It was on the tip of her tongue to angrily demand why he or

one of the soldiers under his command could not show some charity toward this poor ill creature, but then she remembered her plan.

"There was one man," she said very slowly.

He frowned, and she added hastily, "I was on the wharf when John Martin saved this convict's son from drowning." It was on the tip of her tongue to blurt out Timothy Hardy's name, but realized her knowledge would be frowned upon by this small-minded man. "Surely even a hardened criminal would know he owed this man some debt," she added instead.

The lieutenant looked thoughtful. "You may be right, at that." He beamed at her, suddenly all affability. "I'll look into it at once." He bowed and hurried away.

It was still a good hour later, however, before Elizabeth heard the heavy clomp of footsteps outside and hastened to open the door.

The officer who had greeted the coach of convicts on the wharf and who had helped drag John Martin away up the gangplank stood in front of her. He pushed forward a small man and said harshly, "Here's another bit of scum to help you with that bigger one, but why you and the good doctor would go to all this bother I'm sure I don't know, madam."

Elizabeth stood aside for Timothy Hardy to enter, but then slipped between him and the burly soldier. "Thank you, officer, I'll manage fine now."

The sergeant scowled at her and then moved aside to reveal another behind him. "Thought you insisted on the irons coming off, Miss."

"Oh. . .oh, yes of course," she said hastily and gestured for them to enter. She beamed up at him. "How kind! Do thank your lieutenant for me, please. I know God will bless you both for your compassion."

Not even this hardened soldier was immune to her sunny smile. He relaxed and smiled back at her. "Well, reckon they'll all come off soon as the floggin's over today. It kinda unsettles them all, knowing they could be next when they step out of line. There'll be a guard in the corridor at all times," he added with a warning frown at the still figure of Timothy Hardy.

Elizabeth smiled back as pleasantly as she could, and as soon as the fetters had been removed from both of the convicts, thankfully ushered the two men out. Only then did she turn and speak to the small man staring wonderingly from her to John Martin.

"Now, sir," she said briskly, "this brave man is very ill because he saved your son. We have work to do to make sure he survives for you to thank him."

"Oh, I've already done that, madam." The man's voice was soft and cultured like his wife's. "And I've countless times already thanked God for this man."

She smiled approvingly at him. "Good. I have certainly been praying for you both as well as your wife and small son ever since I met them on the wharf, Mr. Hardy."

He stiffened as though shot. "My wife, madam? She was there to see me off?"

The sudden pleading light and dawning hope in his eyes made her smile a little mistily at him. "Yes, she was most certainly there. She told me what a good man you were and how she'd been trying to get permission to say good-bye and even to travel on the ship with you."

Tears filled his eyes. A harsh sob shook his slight frame. "Not a word have I had in weeks. I. . .I thought. . ."

"Your wife spoke very fondly of you, sir."

Despite his tattered appearance, the man seemed to grow in stature before Elizabeth's eyes. It was not just the chains and the journey that had brought him to despair, Elizabeth suddenly realized, but the thought that his wife had turned her back on him.

"Thank you, madam," he said in a much stronger voice. "They dragged me away with all the others when John here went into the water after young Tim. We think they must have been afraid others would jump overboard to try and escape. I didn't even know if my son and John were safe until they threw him down the hold after us. But not a letter, not even a message have I had from my dear wife since I wrote and told her I would be transported on this ship."

What an inhumane system this was to not even pass on letters or messages! Compassion raced through Elizabeth. She reached out her hand and touched his shoulder. "She told me she had sent you a coat, so I'm sure she must have written to you. I can assure you that she still cares for you very much—even asked me to write to her about how you get on while I'm with you on this ship."

"No!"

Elizabeth removed her hand as though stung.

"Please," Timothy said hoarsely, "You mustn't tell her all the horror. She will only be even more devastated. I. . ." He bowed his head and added softly, "I'm too ashamed."

Elizabeth stared at him sadly. Obviously even these first few days on board had been a nightmare to this man, and he expected much worse to come.

"I'll be very careful," she assured him softly.

A harsh cough brought both their heads around to the bunk crowded against the wall.

"Now," she said steadily, "let's make John more comfortable."

Timothy moved swiftly forward as John cried out and moved restlessly. He stopped short as the sick man suddenly opened his eyes and cried out, "Beth, where are you? Beth, I need you desperately! Father! Father, where are you. . . ?"

His voice faded away into incoherent muttering, and Timothy and Elizabeth looked at each other.

Then Elizabeth brushed angrily at the tears that had flooded her eyes at the utter despair that had been in the weak, croaky voice. "We have much work to do, Mr. Hardy. And as we work, we must pray. He must live!"

"Aye," responded Timothy softly. "They say he's a murderer, but whatever he's done, he's still deep down a good man. I've already been praying for him." He hesitated and then looked directly at Elizabeth. "He's a soul in dreadful torment and despair, but he still. . .he still cares about others."

Elizabeth stared back at him for a moment and then turned swiftly away. "And now we must care for him," she whispered softly.

There were many times during the following long hours that Elizabeth was grateful it was Timothy Hardy alone who was there to hear more of the tortured ramblings. Many of his words were in a foreign language Timothy thought was Spanish.

At one stage, it was obvious John Martin was reliving his trial. Then he shouted something out that made Timothy and Elizabeth look at each other. Her eyes were wide, filled with questions.

Timothy nodded slowly at last. "I. . .I've been wondering. . ." he started to say and then had to leap forward as their patient started trying to sit up and was at risk of toppling over.

They didn't speak again. It seemed an intrusion to be forced to listen to the private life and mind of this man, even more so to discuss what he said. Most of it they could make little sense of anyway, but he did rave on and on about a woman called Beth.

The first time he called out, "Elizabeth!" she thought he was calling her, but then he muttered, "no, no, not her. Beth . . .why?" She guessed the woman he called had the same name as herself. He didn't mention his father again, but muttered angry words about someone called Percival and a Lord Farnley. Then even his voice ceased, and he lay deeply unconscious. The exhausted doctor paid a quick visit later on in the day. He shook his head, commended their efforts, and then stumbled away for some well-earned sleep himself.

All through that day and far into the night, death hovered very close in the small cabin. Elizabeth and Timothy fought it with everything they could. When Elizabeth discovered that Timothy's faith in God was, like hers, a deep personal relationship with Him, they even prayed together for the ill convict.

Sometimes the large body shivered and shook. They piled

blankets on, but it wasn't long before the fever would return worse than ever. Then they sponged the large body down with cool water. Elizabeth was glad of Timothy's help as they forced down the many sips of water and then the medicines the doctor had left for them.

As early morning light at last filtered through the small port-hole, they were both exhausted. Timothy was dozing on the other bunk at Elizabeth's insistence. She had already taken her turn to rest only briefly, more to stop Timothy's fussing over her than anything. But she had been unable to sleep and very quickly had resumed her vigil beside John Martin.

She left her hand on the man's hand so she would feel him stir and wearily leaned her head back against the wall. Closing her eyes she whispered, "Oh, Lord, we've done everything we can for this brave man. Please save him."

She hesitated and then added urgently, "Timothy said this man's very angry at You for letting him be imprisoned when he says he's not guilty of any wrong and swore at him every time he tried to mention You. I don't know if he knows about You loving him so much You sent Jesus to die for him."

Tired tears seeped from her closed eyes. Her own relation-ship with God was still very new. "Please don't let him die before he believes in You," she added simply.

The hand beneath hers jerked, and her eyes swung down to her patient. Blue eyes were watching her. For the first time they were really seeing her, and for a moment she was speechless as she stared back at him.

Then the tears started streaming down her face. There were large beads of perspiration on his forehead. Dr. Richmond had told them if that happened it would be a very good sign that his body was fighting the infection in his lungs.

Besides all that, and despite the dazed look that now entered those incredible blue eyes, she knew that for the first time he was truly conscious of her and his surroundings.

three

The angel was still there. She was praying, and she also sounded as though she was. . .was crying!

John frowned. Angels weren't supposed to cry. Angels were supposed to. . . Well, he wasn't quite sure what angels were supposed to do, but certainly crying wasn't one of them. He must be dreaming again.

He started to let his eyes drift shut once more, but they flew open as a soft voice exclaimed, "Oh, you're awake."

This time the beautiful face was transfigured by the most glorious smile he had ever seen. He stared at her, drinking his fill. Then something gently touched him, and he realized she was wiping his forehead.

"Where? What?" Was that croak really his voice?

"Shh," he was told as he felt the feather touch of a finger on his sore lips. "Don't try to talk yet. You've been very sick, but. . ."

The voice faltered and stopped, and he wished it wouldn't. It was filled with warmth and loving care. There had been so little of that in his life so far. Only Beth. . .

Beth!

He struggled to sit up and hardly felt the firm hands that tried to prevent him. Was that horror all a dream, or was this the dream? Suddenly he couldn't breath and started to cough.

"Timothy!"

There was distress in the angel's voice. Vaguely he knew he'd met someone recently called by that name, and then a familiar face loomed over him.

"It's okay, my friend," deep tones told him from a thin face filled with a wide smile. "Don't try and move yet."

John tried to relax at the firm command, and the coughing

fit gradually subsided. He continued to stare unbelievingly at the woman beside Timothy.

"Hold him up a little please, Timothy, and I'll give him another pillow so he can have a drink."

Angrily he gritted his teeth and tried to sit up, but he discovered it took too much effort and was glad of the strong arm that came around him.

Then the woman's delicate perfume was all around him again. This time he knew it was no dream. A cup was held to his lips, and he gulped down the fluid thirstily. It cleared the last fog from his mind, and when he rested his head back on the soft pillow, he allowed his gaze to sweep around the room. He wished it would stop moving up and down.

Then he remembered.

He was on board a ship taking him to the Great Southland for the rest of his miserable life. Bitterness, anger, and despair had been his constant companions since he had walked stiffly from that friendless, crowded courtroom. They crashed in on him again, stronger than ever.

"I've been sick, you say? Then why didn't you let me die?"

The eyes of the woman widened. A flash of anger filled them. "I thought you were a very brave man, John Martin, but only cowards wish they were dead!"

Then he knew he'd seen her before. That old woman had called her Elizabeth. She had been looking at them with such a wondering look on her face as though convicts were some different kind of species from the rest of the human race.

He had been angry that his pulse had taken a great leap at the sound of the name Elizabeth. That had been her full name. Then, when he had known he was wrong, he had sunk to even greater depths of despair. For one ridiculous moment he had thought that at last Beth had come to say good-bye, to perhaps give him some hope that this was all a nightmare he would one day be able to wake from.

He stared back at Elizabeth and said harshly, "When a man has nothing left in life to hope for or have faith in, isn't it time he was allowed to die, madam?"

She gave a very distressed sound, but a wave of exhaustion was closing his eyes. Just as sleep claimed him, he muttered, "Besides, angels should be waiting at heaven's gate, not crying."

Elizabeth stared at him. He was delirious again. She looked worriedly up at Timothy and was immensely relieved when he chuckled.

"When a man recognizes a beautiful woman, he's certainly on the mend." Then his smile faded. "I'd say it's going to be a lot harder to bring healing to his soul than his body."

For a moment she wasn't sure whether to laugh or cry as she stared down at the still form of John Martin. She had the weirdest feeling that such a state of mind could become quite common around this man. He stirred something to life in her that had never been touched by all the gentlemen her aunt had begun parading past her these last few months, in an attempt, so Elizabeth had shrewdly suspected, to fasten her interest and stop her desire to return to Australia.

John slept deeply the rest of that day, only rousing a little at various intervals when they insisted he swallow the tea and broth the ship's cook had been cajoled by Elizabeth into providing.

Dr. Richmond called late that evening and examined his patient. "You're right, Elizabeth. I do believe he is starting to improve at last."

Elizabeth had been worried by the long periods during which the once strong body had been so motionless. Timothy had tried to assure her that John Martin had exhausted himself caring for other convicts before becoming so ill himself. He had not added that no doubt there had been little enough sleep in the cold depths of the prison in Yorkshire, but looking at his own drawn, thin face she gained some inkling of that.

Now she exchanged a delighted smile with Timothy as she asked the doctor, "He is just asleep then, sir, and not still lapsing into unconsciousness?"

She hardly needed to ask, for their patient had stirred briefly while he was being checked, even mumbled about cold hands, before rolling on his side away from them.

The doctor nodded. "His breathing is certainly much better, but there is still considerable congestion in his lungs. It will take several days before he regains much strength."

But the very next day her patient was well enough to try Elizabeth's patience to the limit. He growled at her when she tried to persuade him the doctor had said he was to only have very soft food and was not to be allowed out of bed at all.

"Stop fussing, woman," he snapped at her when she tried to make him more comfortable by shaking up the pillows and the bedclothes.

Woman! Elizabeth opened her mouth to tell him how rude and ungrateful he was, but then something clutched at her heart as she glared into his dark eyes. More than a touch of pain and vulnerability reached through to her before he scowled and looked quickly away.

Suddenly she remembered a time not long after her mother had died. Her father had been confined to the house with a broken leg after a horse had thrown him. He had been a difficult patient too, frustrated and angry at finding himself so helpless.

Adam Stevens, one of her father's stockmen, had seen her tears one day after her father had roared at her to leave him alone.

"A strong man like your father hates to be reminded he can become as helpless physically as anyone," he had told her gently. "He feels humiliated, and it makes him remember other. . .other unpleasant times as well."

Adam was a young convict who had been assigned as a laborer to her father. He had been serving a ten-year sentence for fraud, but her father trusted him, and she had grown very fond of him. It had been the first time she was aware that Adam had known about her father's background.

In case the flood of sympathy that swept through her became visible, Elizabeth turned her back on John. Later that evening she was not so successful in hiding her feelings.

She had briefly left the cabin and on her return found John Martin struggling to stand up. Scowling at him, Timothy was standing with his hands on his hips.

She gave a startled gasp of protest, and Timothy said grimly, "He wouldn't listen to me when I told him Dr. Richmond said he was to stay in bed at least another couple of days—even swore at me."

Elizabeth hesitated uncertainly. Then the large figure swayed and, even as Timothy reached out to steady him, started to cough. It was one of the worst bouts he'd had. Quickly she moved and pumped up the pile of pillows. The moment the coughing subsided, she ordered briskly, "Swing his legs back up, Timothy."

By that time the dark head was leaning on Timothy as though the last scrap of strength had been drained from him. He was beyond protesting as they helped him to lie back once more. As his head flopped back on the pillows and his eyes closed, Elizabeth was distressed at how much his large frame was trembling.

It had been a long, exhausting night and day. Tears welled up in her eyes. She stiffened and fought them back, but a sob broke from her. She swiftly started to turn away, but his eyes had flown open and a trembling hand reached out and grabbed her shoulder.

Elizabeth wasn't quite sure why she couldn't stop the tears from flowing, but she raised her chin defiantly when she realized he was staring at her with absolute amazement.

She dashed away the tears angrily. "So, sir, you so despise the care I. . .we have taken of you that you are in a hurry to return to your luxury quarters in the hold!"

Then she was ashamed of taking refuge in her anger as his face lost every bit of color it had gained the last few hours.

"That's the second time you've cried." His voice was barely audible. "I'm. . .I'm sorry, Elizabeth. . .Miss Waverley. . ."

His face had softened. Gone was that cold, hard look that

always somehow hurt something deep inside her. She felt herself softening toward him but shrugged off his hand and turned toward Timothy.

"It's been perfectly obvious for hours that our patient is going to behave exactly as he pleases. I'm tired," she added abruptly. "I believe I'll have my meal in the dining room after all. It's quite clear you don't need me here."

As she swept toward the door, Elizabeth was proud that her voice had held not the slightest tremor.

๛

Silence filled the cabin after the door had snapped closed behind Elizabeth. Neither man moved.

Then Timothy grunted, picked up a plate from the tray, and plonked it down next to John. "Well, guess that gives the two of us three meals," he snapped.

John stared down at the food. A few moments ago he had been hungry. Now he felt too sick at heart to be bothered eating. Elizabeth could not have given him more tender care if she had been his sister—or his wife.

He shook his head. How had that thought crept past the guard he had been trying to keep in place all day! But the touch, the sweetness of her had been inescapable from that first moment he had opened his eyes.

John stared at the food. He looked up at the little man who had proved over and over how much he cared about him. Timothy was looking down so miserably at his own plate that at last John started to eat. Then his appetite kicked in again, and it wasn't long before both men were finished.

"I suppose we'd better enjoy this luxury while we can," Timothy sighed, expressing the thought on both men's minds.

John looked around the room. "It's amazing that we've even been allowed in here at all."

"Dr. Richmond insisted, said he didn't want to lose your help with the other men," Timothy said quietly. He hesitated and then added firmly, "But the least you can do is treat Elizabeth with more courtesy and respect. She's a good woman."

John was silent for a long moment. "I became too friendly once with a 'good woman.'" His low voice was filled with bitterness. "If she'd been a woman straight from the gutter, it couldn't have ended up any worse."

"You've mentioned this Beth a couple times," Timothy said encouragingly. "Was she the woman who caused such problems?"

ॐ

Elizabeth had discovered that everyone who was capable of eating in the dining room had already done so by the time she arrived. Her anger had faded, but her appetite had been very poor. After forcing herself to eat a few mouthfuls, she slowly made her way back to the cabin.

The cabin door was slightly open, and she stood still in the passageway as she heard Timothy's question. She held her breath as she waited for John's answer.

ॐ

John's laugh was harsh. "Yes. Not that she seemed so terrible. She was always going on about the church and the local minister and how wonderful he was."

He was silent for a long moment. "I met Beth Rivers one day when her horse had cast a shoe. I had been in England for several weeks but had only a few days before managed to get a job on the Farnley estate working with Jock, the game-keeper. I was feeling especially lonely that beautiful spring morning, and she was the most beautiful woman. . ."

He paused and swallowed. "We became good friends in the next few weeks. I thought she was my only real friend in all of England. She said her mother was sick, and she was worried and lonely too. We. . ." He flushed slightly, but lifted his head proudly.

"One day in the woods we. . .I. . .my feelings became too much for me and we. . .I kissed her, and she kissed me back."

He looked swiftly up at Timothy. When he merely raised an enquiring eyebrow, John smiled slightly. "I know," he said softly, "it was just one kiss, but Beth did not think so." He sighed. "Perhaps it was then I fully realized just how young and inexperienced she was."

Timothy did not move. After taking a deep breath, John continued in a low voice. "I know now I was just reaching out because I felt so alone, but then I thought our friendship might be turning into something deeper. Her reaction shook me. She. . .she was shocked, horrified. She felt that if anyone had seen us she would be compromised. She was so upset that I. . .I very foolishly burst out that if that had happened, I'd marry her."

He was silent for a moment and then sighed. "I know now I did not love her, and it was a very foolish thing to do for just one kiss, but. . .but it was then I found out who she really was. She was scared someone might have seen Lord Farnley's stepdaughter kissing the offsider to his lordship's gamekeeper. Apparently she had kept her own father's name when her mother had married Lord Farnley, the man I had come all the way from Spain to find. He. . .he. . ."

John looked up wearily at Timothy. "It's a long story, but he is my father, and by that time I had almost decided to approach him and show him the Bible, my mother's letters, tell him I was his son. But I had been stupid enough to compromise his stepdaughter with secret meetings and then that kiss."

"Your father's a lord!"

At the stunned look on Timothy's face, John gave a harsh laugh. "Hard to believe? Yes, it was for me too when I found out. I don't want to talk about him."

Timothy looked very troubled but kept silent. John stirred restlessly and then continued.

"Of course Beth wanted to know why I was so upset, and I couldn't tell her. I mumbled some excuse and left her there in the wood. A few minutes later I found Jock's body. He had been killed some time beforehand, while I was with Beth."

Timothy raised his head sharply. "So she could have testified you were with her?"

John nodded grimly. "At first I didn't say anything about

her. It didn't seem right to involve her, but then when I realized how serious it all was, I wrote to her several times. I begged her, pleaded with her to come forward and verify my story, but she never did. The prosecution just read out a note from her saying she had not seen me that day and asking to be excused personal testimony as her mother was very ill."

He laughed harshly again. "Perhaps I may have been starting to fall in love with her, perhaps I was only beginning to hope I was lovable, that there was someone in the world who could love me. She was so sweet, had told me she really liked me and wanted to be my friend you see, and I had believed her. I have acknowledged she was very young, but I believed she cared for me and that we were good enough friends for her to at the very least do what she could to save my life. But apparently her precious honor was more important to her than saving a humble workman from the hangman's noose."

Neither man spoke for a while, and then Timothy said quietly, "I'd say Elizabeth Waverley is a woman straight from heaven." His voice held reverence.

John raised his head and stared bleakly at the man who was fast becoming his friend. "She was praying for me when I was sick, wasn't she?"

Timothy hesitated briefly, and then he said directly, "We were both praying for you, separately as well as together, and God has partly answered our prayer."

As he stared back at him, John felt something cold and hard deep inside him ease. During all these miserable months he had thought there was no one left in the whole world who cared whether he lived or died. And now here was this little man telling him. . .

"We believed you were very close to not waking up again," Timothy added very softly, "and despite your wish that you had died, I for one am very glad you're on the mend, and I know she really cares also."

John swallowed rapidly. "I. . .I can't afford to let anyone care for me, and I certainly can't let myself love. . .care for anyone, especially a woman." Suddenly he looked directly at Timothy and asked quietly, "How long is your sentence?"

Timothy scowled. "I told you that first day. Ten years." He added abruptly, "It does no good dwelling on it. What about you?"

"Life."

John saw Timothy wince and close his eyes briefly. He gave a harsh laugh and looked at the ceiling. "So you see, there's not much point in anyone caring what happens to me. I've been told numerous times by various guards, soldiers, and even other prisoners that I was lucky not to have been hung. Instead, I'm at the mercy of England's penal system until the day I die, and we've both already had a taste of that. From what we've heard and seen, it can only get worse."

There was silence for a long moment. Weariness washed over John again. "No one believes me when I tell them I've never killed anybody, and no one is ever likely to now."

"Are you a murderer, John Martin?"

The soft voice startled both men. She was standing in the open doorway, watching them. Elizabeth moved slowly forward, not once taking her eyes from John.

John savored her beauty, from the healthy color on her serious face to her dainty feet. Speechless, he looked into her clear, direct eyes as she stopped close to him. *Surely no one could lie to an angel,* he thought helplessly.

"Well, John Martin, do you swear before my Lord Jesus Christ that you have not killed anyone and are undeserving of this incarceration?"

His mind flashed back to the time he had desperately shouted out his innocence in that crowded courtroom. So many times he had already protested his innocence.

He felt as though he could hardly breathe as he returned her gaze. "I swear before God that I am innocent of murder."

He could hear the hopelessness that swept through him echoing in his voice, and he closed his eyes, not wanting to see the disbelief in her beautiful ones.

"Then, John Martin, somehow we are going to have to prove it to the authorities, aren't we?"

His eyes flew open.

A tender smile shone at him.

As he stared unbelievingly at her, the smile widened to a mischievous grin. "I don't believe a delirious man is a good liar. It was a long night, and you told us quite a lot about yourself."

John glanced wildly at Timothy. He also was smiling gently at him. Then John's eyes locked with Elizabeth's, and for the first time a flicker of hope lightened his heart.

As she saw his face lighten, Elizabeth's heart went out to him. She had stood outside the cabin's partly opened door listening, battling tears at his words and heartache. Now she looked away, not willing to let him see her own reaction, and then bustled forward, removed the dinner tray, and placed it out in the corridor before carefully closing the door.

"Let us hope we do not have any unnecessary interruptions," she said briskly as she pulled a chair closer to the bed and looked at both men, who still had not moved. "Now, my father is not a man without some influence in New South Wales, and he may be able to help," she said briskly. "But the first thing we have to do is find out what happened to land you here."

John closed his eyes tightly, and then opened them again to stare unbelievingly first at her and then at Timothy.

After a long moment, Timothy made a helpless gesture with his hands. "We have nothing else to do. Can it do any harm to tell us all about it? What happened after you found the murdered man?"

John's gaze darkened. "I've done nothing but tell what happened over and over again, but no one has believed me. Why should you two?"

Elizabeth looked at him steadily. "Because when you were delirious you called and called someone named Jock, then you said, 'What are you doing there? He's cold, so cold. Dead!

No, no! My knife? No, no, I didn't kill him.'"

Her voice had echoed only some of the expression that had been in the voice that had shocked both his listeners in the dark hours of the night. When he merely stared at her, she continued calmly, "There was a lot more, most of it mumbled words we couldn't make head nor tail of, but you called for your father and. . .and Beth."

Astonishment filled his dark eyes. He gave an unbelieving snort and fell back on the pillows. "Now I know you're insane. There's no way I would have called for my father."

The bitter, angry tone was filled with hate and caused Elizabeth's heart to ache even more. At the same time, a little voice inside her acknowledged that he had not refuted calling for the woman named Beth, the woman she had just over-heard him say he had kissed. Suddenly she wondered if that kiss had been so hungry, so passionate from a love-starved man that it had frightened the inexperienced girl he had por-trayed Beth to be. Perhaps that had been another reason the young woman would have been so upset.

Timothy and Elizabeth glanced at each other. She saw her own sadness reflected in his face before she turned back to the large figure on the bed. Timothy had a son whom he loved dearly and who loved him. Her own father was a silent, taciturn man, but she had never doubted his great love for her. Yet for some reason, John hated his father.

She said gently, "Sir, I'm not sure how long we have before we are interrupted or even before you must return to. . .to. . ." She bit her lip, hating to think of the conditions both men would be returned to eventually. Hastily she added, "Could you at least tell us where you come from? Your voice has an accent neither of us have been able to place."

John opened his eyes and stared blindly in front of him. Suddenly he could see the bright sunshine of the corner of Spain he had grown up in and longed passionately to be back there in its warmth and light. He heard his grandmother's gentle voice insisting to her angry husband that with all his other studies, their only daughter's son must learn to speak and read English properly, "like she would have wished."

How glad he had been that the old lady had lived until he was old enough to understand that she had insisted on those lessons because his father had been an English soldier, an important man, an officer. Then she had died, and there had only been the bitter old man who had always hated him, as well as the uncles and cousins who had made his life as miserable as they could.

The memories flooded back. "My mother was Spanish, and I lived in Spain all my life until my grandfather died a few weeks before I went to England," he said abruptly at last. "To my utter amazement he left me a very large amount of money. Of all his grandsons, I was the only one who had worked hard beside him on his prosperous farm. He had always treated me harshly, but in his will he did what he thought was fair. He left all the property to my uncles and cousins. The very day of the funeral they made it clear I no longer had a home.

"That same night, while I was wondering where to go and what I should do, my mother's sister crept into my room and gave me a small box. She told me she had kept the contents hidden for her beloved sister. All my life she had been afraid her father would only burn them as he had destroyed everything else belonging to the daughter who had dared to marry an English soldier and then died giving birth to his son.

"And. . .and she told me that my father had not been killed at Waterloo as I had always been told. He had returned, but he left me with them. She clammed up after that and raced off as though she regretted giving me even that information."

John gave a harsh sound that could have been a laugh. "All my life the old man had led me to believe my parents had never married. Suddenly I was told my mother and father had been married after all, but he had not wanted me and had left me with that awful family."

"What was in the box?" Elizabeth asked quietly after he had been silent for some time.

"Letters from my father to my mother and a small English family Bible."

"A family Bible!" exclaimed the fascinated Elizabeth. "But. . .but surely that would have had your father's family tree in it and would have been a treasured possession for a soldier to give away."

Surprise crossed his face, and then he looked thoughtful. "You English do seem to put great honor on your Bible. Even in your courts—"

Suddenly he started to cough again. They managed to get him to sip more of the medicine, but it was a while before the paroxysm passed.

"Perhaps you should rest now, John, and tell us more later," Elizabeth said gently.

"No," he gasped. "Be. . .right. . .soon."

Elizabeth insisted he have more of the medicine the good doctor had left to soothe the coughing attacks. When his breathing had returned to normal and he was resting quietly at last, she asked, "Was there anything in the letters that could prove you were his son?"

"He called her Sophia, his beloved wife, and was so thrilled John Harold had arrived safely."

His voice was harsh, and Elizabeth clenched her fists at the pain in his face.

"All those years I had been called Martinez, my mother's name, but here was proof that he had married my mother. My first instinct was to wave it in front of all those who had despised me for so many years. But then I knew the money and the letters were like a ticket to freedom. They had always hated me, and I didn't want to have anything to do with any of them anymore."

He stopped and looked angrily at Elizabeth and Timothy. "Freedom! It led to pain I never dreamed could exist!"

Elizabeth swallowed, trying to get rid of the lump that had lodged in her throat. As he had been talking, she had pictured the boy he must have been, growing up in such an unloving atmosphere. Those brilliant blue eyes alone must have made him stand out amongst his dark-eyed cousins and been a constant reminder to his family of his origins.

She wanted passionately to assure him that one day he would be free, that there must be some way the real murderer could be found. She put her hand on his, but he flung it aside. A humiliating blush spread swiftly up her cheeks before she realized that he wasn't even looking at her, his tormented thoughts in another place, another time.

"At first when I arrived in England it was all so exciting," he continued in a weary voice. "It was easy enough to find out the name of the regiment that had been stationed in my family's village near Salamanca during the Peninsula War against Napoleon. Even finding out someone who had known this man called Harold Farnley was easy, but that's when it all became so impossible. He wasn't just an ordinary soldier. My aunt had been right. He was an officer, but even more than that he now was Lord Farnley, a wealthy land owner, married with another family.

"Tell me, how can you bounce up to someone like that and tell him you're the son he abandoned more than twenty years before?" John lifted his head and glared once again at his two intent listeners.

Neither moved. After a long pause Elizabeth said in a low, choked voice, "Some hurt, angry men would have no problem at all doing that."

"And where would it have got me?" He subsided again onto the pillow. Suddenly he hammered his fist on the mattress furiously. His voice rose. "Tell me, what kind of man would turn his back on his own son and never try to contact him? I had to find out what kind of man my father was. I managed to get a job on the estate. I had to get to know this Lord Farnley and see if I wanted to have anything to do with such a one!"

Elizabeth sprang anxiously to her feet to hush him, but it was too late. The door flew open. Lieutenant Edwards strode angrily into the room.

four

The next morning Elizabeth wasted no time in having a sketchy wash, dressing, and hurrying back to the cabin next to the doctor's. There had been no time for further talking among the three friends the previous night. Dr. Richmond had entered the room just as they were trying to make light of John's outburst to the suspicious officer.

He had succeeded in getting rid of the lieutenant for them, but he had also ordered Elizabeth to her own cabin with the firm words, "There is no need for you to stay any longer this evening. I'll give our patient something to help him sleep, and if there are any problems, Mr. Hardy will be able to send word to me."

In truth, she was very tired and had been glad of the privacy of her own cabin. She had prayed fervently and then fallen into a deep sleep the moment her head had touched the pillow.

Now she was eager for John to tell them the rest of his story so that somehow they could work out how to go about proving his innocence.

"Ah, Elizabeth, up early I see."

She paused as the doctor's voice greeted her from his open doorway. "Have you seen your patient this morning, sir?" she asked eagerly.

He looked at her a little strangely and then said quietly, "Come in and say good morning to Mrs. Richmond, my dear. I'm pleased to say she is much better now."

Elizabeth hesitated for a moment and then said with a slight smile, "I'm very glad to hear that, sir, but I was actually referring to your John Martin."

"Come in, and I'll tell you how he is."

45

Elizabeth found herself being escorted firmly into the doctor's cabin. Something about the doctor's demeanor frightened her.

"Is. . .is something wrong?"

"No, no," he hastened to reassure her.

"So there you are, young lady. I do think you could have spent some time with me yesterday."

The querulous voice was filled with indignation, and Elizabeth hurried to greet Mrs. Richmond.

Her rather flustered protestations were interrupted by the doctor, who said briskly, "I've already told you, my dear, that this kind young lady has been good enough to help me with a convict who was very close to death."

"And very unsuitable that was. Truly, Dr. Richmond, I don't know what you could have been thinking of to allow a gently nurtured young lady like Elizabeth anywhere near one of those dreadful men. I don't know what her father will have to say of our care of her!"

"Oh, but they weren't—"

"The man would have died without her, madam." Dr. Richmond threw Elizabeth a warning glance.

Reluctantly she subsided, knowing only too well the damage her reputation would receive in many circles if she were known to have befriended a convict, let alone two of them. More importantly any gossip could hurt her dear father.

"Now," he continued with a warm smile, "I called you in to say a big thank you for your help and to tell you that our patient is well enough to have been returned to his own bunk."

Elizabeth stared at him in absolute dismay. Then she realized his smile did not reach his eyes and that he was watching her closely.

With a tremendous effort she forced a smile. "Good news, indeed, sir, but last night he was still very sick with the most dreadful cough. I must confess I do believe a couple more days' care would have been most beneficial."

"Well, your patient didn't agree with you in the least," Mrs.

Richmond snapped. "Apparently he agreed to go quite readily. Rather surprised the lieutenant this morning, I must say. He said he thought the fellow would protest most vigorously. That other strange little man said he'd look after him. Now, do let's stop talking about those poor creatures. We wanted to talk to you about various activities that are organized on this ship from time to time to help the journey pass as quickly as possible."

Elizabeth tried her best to join in the older woman's chatter. The depth of her disappointment stunned her, but she valiantly tried not to let it show. Once or twice she saw the good doctor watching her and managed to smile at him brightly.

He soon showed her that she had not succeeded in fooling him. When he at last ushered her from the cabin, informing her abruptly that they could both do with some exercise on deck, he said directly, "Your patient will certainly not be as comfortable in those cramped quarters in the hold as he was under your care, Elizabeth, but you need not worry unnecessarily about the convicts. This may be only a converted merchant ship fitted out with the necessary berths and security devices to ship convicts instead of cargo, but I make sure all convicts under my care receive the best treatment I can obtain for them."

He paused and frowned as he studied her face. "You really must forget about the convicts, my dear Elizabeth. Your father would not like to know you have had any contact with them at all."

She stiffened proudly and stared steadily back at him. "John Martin is a good man, sir. He has sworn he is innocent, and I believe him."

Alarm filled the older man's face. "Do not be so foolish, madam!" he said angrily. "All convicts protest their innocence."

She was silent for a long moment, then asked quietly, "Did my father, sir?"

Shock widened his eyes. Then they narrowed, and he said softly, "Be very careful, Elizabeth. My friend believes you are unaware of his past and would be most upset if he knew. I have never spoken of it even to my wife."

Elizabeth's mother had told her that her father had been imprisoned at Port Arthur in Van Dieman's Land for most of his ten-year sentence. Then he had worked on properties west of Sydney before managing to obtain a grant of land for himself when he had completed his sentence. Her mother had been the daughter of an important, wealthy family he had worked for and from the start had been intrigued by the stern but kind young man. Against her family's wishes she had married the still young, hard-working emancipist.

"He had been so hurt by life and yet could still smile at the world. I fell in love with him," her mother had told her simply, but with such a soft glow of love in her eyes that the young Elizabeth had vowed there and then never to marry anyone she could not love like that.

And it was obvious to all that the rather stern man adored the woman who in his eyes had deigned to love someone so far beneath her. Shortly after they married, they had moved west of the ranges. The few people in that vast land did not know about his past. Then the surgeon had taken up land bordering his property.

According to her mother, Dr. Richmond had recognized Elizabeth's father from his own brief time at Port Arthur and had at first kept his distance. Fortunately the good doctor had believed that everyone should have an opportunity to put his past behind him.

Over the years as they battled the harsh land to establish their properties, a deep trust and friendship had grown between the two men from such different backgrounds. Perhaps it was because each knew the horrors of the convict system even though that knowledge had been from such different perspectives.

"Sometimes I think both men need each other to talk to about those days," her mother had told her daughter with a sad look. "There are times when the nightmares return. He will never speak of them to me, but he has been so much better since knowing Dr. Richmond."

Dr. Richmond had turned away, staring across the rolling deep blue waves for a long moment. "To answer your question, Elizabeth," he said at last, "no, I've never once heard him protest his innocence, but he has been punished for what he did as a very young man. He was born and bred in some of the worst slums in London, where men do anything they must in order to survive. I have always admired tremendously the way he has so successfully made a new life for himself."

He looked back at her steadily. "Australia has been the land of opportunity for many a convict who has been brave enough to work hard and put the past behind him. I honor your father for the man he has become, and I am proud to call him my friend."

Elizabeth's eyes moistened. "And I am very proud he is my father, sir. I love him dearly."

"Then I know you'll do naught to hurt him, my dear." With that the doctor smiled at her, bowed, and strode swiftly away.

Elizabeth looked after him, her eyes blinded with tears. Then she turned and grasped the rail and stared out across the water to the endless horizon.

The doctor was right, her father would be angry if she told him of her association and growing liking for the two convicts, especially John. The way he had tried to stop her from becoming too friendly with any of the assigned convicts who had worked for him from time to time, the way he had hurried her past any chain gang they had been unable to avoid passing, his reluctance to even mention the penal system in her presence had been a part of her life as long as she could remember.

As she had grown older she had not been able to understand what had amounted almost to an obsession on his part at times. She had defied him on several occasions, causing friction between them until her worried mother had disclosed her father's convict past, making Elizabeth solemnly promise never to mention to him that she knew.

"Foolishly, he is so bitterly ashamed of what living in the London slums made him. He was only a boy when he was sentenced as a pickpocket, but he has never been a bad man. He only wants to protect you from all evil," the gentle voice had told her. But it had been the unfailing love and respect and admiration her mother had always shown for him, as well as Elizabeth's own respect for her big, loving father, that had made her try to keep her promise all these years.

Deep in thought Elizabeth began to pace slowly along the deck, only vaguely aware of the attention she was attracting from several of the crew and soldiers. Surely her father would be sympathetic to someone who had been wrongly convicted. Perhaps he too had met someone over the years whom he had believed could have been innocent. But how could she gain his support for John Martin—or Martinez or Farnley or whatever the man's name was, she wondered a little crossly.

Someone nearby delicately cleared his throat. "Ah, my dear Miss Waverley."

She started and turned her head. "Lieutenant Edwards," she acknowledged with a dignified nod.

"I'm. . .er. . .glad your reprehensible task is at an end and we can now see you taking the air."

Elizabeth looked quickly around her and was made aware that several people were now within earshot. A toothless old man in the convict gray uniform was swabbing the deck nearby.

As the surgeon-superintendent of the *Royal Lady*, Dr. Richmond had ensured as many convicts as possible were given work, knowing that besides the usual privations of food and fresh air on a long sea voyage, the main problem was boredom. Much unrest was prevented when the convicts were given something to do. The convicts swabbed, scrubbed, and laundered, taking as much menial work off the crew's shoulders as possible.

The old man gave Elizabeth a furtive, toothless smile. He had so greeted her cheerfully—yet respectfully—several times before, and she smiled back before returning her gaze to the lieutenant.

He was glaring at the old man. Afraid the man would suffer

for her friendliness, Elizabeth quickly moved forward so that her body hid him from view. "It is certainly a beautiful day, Lieutenant," she said brightly with a gurgle of laughter, "and do you think my father's old friend would really give me a difficult task? He was merely saving me from boredom so early on our voyage. But thank you for your concern," she added demurely.

To her amusement his chest seemed to literally puff up. He affectedly tugged at the cuff of his scarlet uniform jacket and held out his arm, which was bent at the elbow. "Shall we promenade, Miss Waverley?"

She managed not to smile at his pomposity. Did one "promenade" on board a ship? Thoughtfully she looked at him. It was obvious that Dr. Richmond would not take at all kindly to being quizzed from time to time about the convicts. Quickly she decided this slight young man would be as good a source of information as any during the long sea voyage, so she only hesitated briefly before taking the proffered arm.

In the days and weeks that followed, Elizabeth often regretted her impulse to accept the lieutenant's friendly overtures during the walk around the deck that morning. Unfortunately Lieutenant Edwards was the kind of man who believed that no woman of good taste and breeding could fail to be enamored with him.

There were times when she could have screamed with boredom as he talked on about himself and his future aspirations. She bore it all for the snippets of information about the convicts that he at times let slip after light encouragement.

It wasn't until Mrs. Richmond spoke to her one evening that Elizabeth imagined she might have a more serious problem.

"Oh, how exciting it must be for you, my dear Elizabeth," that good lady said soulfully.

Since Elizabeth had just spent the past hour listening to the lieutenant telling her for what seemed the hundredth time about his family's wonderful mansion in beautiful Devon, she was completely at sea.

"Madam?"

The ship had sailed to the Tropics, and both ladies used their fans in the midday heat. Mrs. Richmond paused, looked at Elizabeth keenly for a moment, and then laughed. She tapped her on the wrist with her fan, before vigorously waving it again to try and make the hot, humid air more bearable.

"Oh, don't think I'm too old to remember how it was when a handsome young man was courting me."

Elizabeth had become quite fond of Mrs. Richmond despite her talkative nature. She smiled at her gently. "Oh, I'm sure you must remember quite a few beaus before you met your husband."

Faint color touched the lined face. "For sure, my dear, for sure, but until my dear Dr. Richmond, none courted me as earnestly as your young man."

"My young man!" Elizabeth stared in horror.

A picture flew into her mind of a broad shouldered, tall man with jet black, curly hair who gazed at her so directly from deep blue eyes. Surely Mrs. Richmond did not know of the times she had been able not only to catch glimpses of him doing the various tasks assigned to him, but also stopped to speak to him! Even that morning she had been thrilled to see that he had looked a much better color.

"It's very obvious that Lieutenant Edwards will seek out your father as soon as he can to—"

"Lieutenant Edwards! You think that he. . .I. . .? Mrs. Richmond! No, no you are sadly mistaken," she said sharply. "Besides, he must know that I have not encouraged him in the least."

Mrs. Richmond let her fan drop and frowned. "Well, I don't know how you could say that when you spend so much time with him each day, and I must say it does you no credit to raise false hopes in him."

"But. . .but I haven't raised false hopes. Why, surely I have spent no more time with him than. . .than with you or

Dr. Richmond," Elizabeth protested rapidly. "Surely you realize that the captain and his officers have been too busy to spend time with any of us, and on a ship how can we avoid anyone when there are so few. . .well so few we are allowed to associate with," she added, "especially since your husband is so adamant about no longer having me help him with the convicts."

Mrs. Richmond sniffed and stared at her disapprovingly, but to the embarrassed Elizabeth's relief, the woman did not refer to the matter again.

However Elizabeth was sufficiently alarmed by the conversation that she made sure she was more reserved with the lieutenant from that moment on. While remaining polite, she spoke briefly and rather coldly to him. Several times she saw chagrin, and once such a dreadful flare of anger burned in his cold eyes that for a brief moment she was afraid. She suddenly realized how mistaken she had been in thinking this man was delicate. There was a dark, cold side to him that he usually kept well hidden beneath his soft, flattering exterior. She prayed much about the whole matter, but something deep within her withdrew even further from the man.

Then she found out that when the lieutenant was not happy, those under his command were made miserable also.

The ship stopped only briefly at Capetown on the coast of Africa to replenish supplies and fresh food and water. It was a delight to see Table Mountain gradually come out of hiding as the clouds around it dispersed, to see the forests and brilliant blooms of geraniums and roses after all the weeks of staring across the expanse of the empty sea.

Elizabeth thoroughly enjoyed her first trip ashore, even though once she put foot to solid ground the earth seemed to heave and move. After weeks of the constantly rolling motion of the ship, it suddenly seemed as though the hard ground was unstable and the ship so firm. It did not take her long to gain her land legs again, and she and Mrs. Richmond gladly went off to see all they could of the bustling port town.

However, on returning to the ship they were dismayed to find a very angry doctor. Despite all Dr. Richmond's protests, the captain insisted on keeping the convicts locked below deck while in port.

"Captain Longman's hands are tied," he angrily confided to Elizabeth and his wife. "Lieutenant Edwards has given shore leave to most of the men under his command and left too few to guard the convicts above deck. The ship's crew are frantically busy securing and loading the ship. The conditions below deck are dreadful. It's too hot, not enough fresh air, and I'm afraid—"

He stopped abruptly, apparently realizing he should not be alarming the two women, but Elizabeth was consumed with worry. She hastened to her cabin and threw herself on her knees.

"Oh, Lord, protect John and Timothy from evil. Keep them strong and. . .and safe. Help Dr. Richmond and. . .and help me. . ."

Her voice died away, but she spent much time on her knees until she gained a measure of peace that God was in control of all their lives.

The doctor became busier and busier the next couple days as many convicts succumbed to fever once again in the hot, airless, and foul atmosphere of the hold. A few fights had broken out among the miserable men, and Elizabeth's anxiety increased for John and Timothy. Dr. Richmond steadfastly refused Elizabeth's offers of assistance and instead arranged more excursions ashore for her and his wife to escape the increasing tension on board ship.

Elizabeth did enjoy seeing all she could of the strange sights and sounds of the bustling port, but the ladies found that tension in the town was also high. There was considerable unrest among the Boers. The law abolishing slavery that Britain had passed the previous year had ruined a number of their farmers, and many had decided to leave the cape colony. Thousands of them were planning a journey into the interior to start new lives away from British rule. There was much wild talk, but also fear of the native tribes they would encounter and no doubt upset—especially the fierce Bantu-speaking peoples.

As wonderful as it was to be on dry land again, both women acknowledged their relief by the time the ship sailed. However, there was no immediate relief for the convicts. Most of the soldiers, including Lieutenant Edwards, had unfortunate aftereffects from their nights ashore. Aching heads and bodies meant they were more intolerant than ever of the convicts.

As the ship plowed through the waters of the Indian Ocean toward the west Australian coast, the tension on board continued to mount. Despite both the captain and the doctor's pleas, Lieutenant Edwards remained adamant. The convicts had been behaving far too badly to be allowed out of their dark, dank conditions. They were far easier to control below deck than above, he insisted.

But he was soon proven wrong.

Despite all Dr. Richmond's efforts, the third night out, an elderly convict died. At dawn, when they realized what had happened, the terrified convicts rioted.

Elizabeth was wakened by shouts of alarm and running feet outside her cabin. For a moment she froze. Then she heard a distant, escalating roar of hundreds of angry voices. She offered up frantic prayers for John and Timothy as she quickly flung on her clothes. No one was in sight when she cautiously opened her door and peered out. Suddenly a muffled shot rang out. She took a deep breath and raced to hammer on the door of the doctor's cabin.

"Mrs. Richmond, it's Elizabeth," she called loudly.

The door flew open, and Mrs. Richmond pulled her in, immediately slamming the door shut and locking it.

"Oh, my dear, we have been ordered to stay here until we are told it is safe to leave," she said a little hysterically. "It's as Dr. Richmond warned and warned that arrogant young man. The convicts would only bear so much."

Gradually the distant noise died away except for an occasional loud voice that sounded as though it were issuing orders. Elizabeth was on the verge of ignoring Mrs. Richmond's frantic pleas not to leave the safety of the cabin to find out what was happening when the doctor at last appeared.

His face was pale, his clothes disheveled and streaked with grime. "One convict shot dead and several to face severe penalties," he snapped grimly in response to their anxious faces. Then he hesitated and looked at Elizabeth.

Her heart nearly stopped at his expression of sympathy.

"Your two patients seem to have been in the thick of things. They are among those at this moment being hauled above deck before the captain and the lieutenant. No! Elizabeth—"

But his anger and urgent call did not stop Elizabeth's headlong flight from the cabin. Her heart pounding, she scrambled up the gangway and onto the deck.

five

It seemed as though the whole ship's company was assembling on the deck. A stream of dazed, stumbling convicts were being herded together, guarded closely by grim-lipped soldiers with their rifles at the ready.

Elizabeth stared frantically around and could not stop the cry that burst from her lips. The bruised and bloodied figure of John Martin was swaying slightly amid a small group of convicts slightly apart from the others.

At her cry, Lieutenant Edwards swung around and stared haughtily at her. She stared back at him, not troubling to hide her anger and disgust, letting him see she blamed him for this whole mess.

It was a mistake.

His lips curled in a menacing smile before he turned away and stared thoughtfully at John Martin and Timothy Hardy.

The names of the convicts who were blamed for starting the riot were called out. They included those of Timothy and John. When those two names were read out, Elizabeth gasped and then realized that the lieutenant was watching her, waiting for her response.

However, it appeared that she was not the only one dismayed. She saw Sergeant Hobbs step forward, salute, and speak quietly to his superior officer.

Elizabeth slipped closer, in time to hear him protest a little louder in his rough voice, "But sir, several of my men said that the last few days they have several times managed to calm the others, and today those two helped our soldiers quell the riot."

Something deep inside Elizabeth relaxed. Somehow she had known the two men she still could not help but think of as friends could not have been among the leaders of the riot. Then she tensed at the lieutenant's icy response.

"That's enough, Sergeant! According to a couple convicts, they were among the leaders, and unfortunately for them the only man who could tell us either way is the one I shot dead."

The sergeant hesitated, but then turned abruptly away. Elizabeth saw the anger on his flushed face even as the lieutenant roared out so all could hear, "A Botany Bay dozen to the lot of you! And may it be a lesson to the rest of you miserable scum!"

Groans and cries for mercy came from all quarters, but the tall figure supporting his slight companion said nothing. Elizabeth felt the doctor muffle an exclamation and turned to him, feeling a sense of relief.

"Surely a mere twelve strokes is a relatively mild punishment?" she whispered with some surprise.

He gave a harsh snort and said angrily, "A Botany Bay dozen is not twelve. It's twenty-five, and more than capable of exposing a man's backbone."

Twenty-five lashes! She stared at him and then swung around. "No, no, how could you?" she cried out furiously, "You. . .you. . ."

Impulsively she started forward, only to have her arm grasped firmly and pulled back. "Leave it, Elizabeth," the doctor whispered earnestly in her ear. "You'll only make it worse. If he won't change his mind on the word of his own man, he won't be seen to back down for a woman."

That he was right was made immediately apparent. The lieutenant stared her straight in the eye, and she saw something like triumph in his face as, without taking his eyes from her, he called out harshly, "And change that to fifty each for Timothy Hardy and John Martin as the main instigators."

The grip on her arm tightened, and Elizabeth bit back the horrified protest that sprang to her lips. Not taking her eyes from the lieutenant, she straightened, determined to stare him down, letting him see she knew this for what it was—

petty vengeance on herself.

Still obviously afraid of what she may try to do, the doctor frantically whispered, "The sentences are still relatively light in comparison to those of earlier years. No longer are five hundred given out as in the earlier part of the century. Lashes of twenty-five to one hundred are quite normal. On rare occasions one hundred and fifty are still ordered by magistrates.

"He's probably only ordered such a small number because of the number of convicts involved. He may fear the strength of the scourger may not last the distance." Dr. Richmond added grimly, "Besides, he knows that I have to verify the conditions of the men as they are flogged. I just wish Captain Longman was not so weak as to allow this officer to behave as though he were the main authority on this ship!"

With that, the doctor hurried away to attend to some urgent duties before the floggings commenced. His place was taken by his pale-faced, distressed wife, who urged her charge to retire below deck until the whole miserable business was completed.

Elizabeth looked at her. After a long moment and with a measure of calm that she knew could only come from God, she said quietly, "Mrs. Richmond, I fervently believe that if we as the only two women on board were to stay and witness the events here, it may curb some of the. . .the ferocity of the strokes. But if you find you cannot stay, madam, I must."

The two women had developed a good understanding over the weeks of enforced contact, but not until the older woman stared at her for a long moment and then said quietly, "I agree entirely, my dear," did Elizabeth know that they shared a common strength of purpose.

Only then did Elizabeth allow the tears pressing against her burning eyelids to run down her cheeks. She scrubbed them angrily aside, mentally and spiritually preparing to do battle with anyone who would seek to order them away. She also understood that she would need all her strength to be able to witness the horror of what was about to happen.

She saw Dr. Richmond refrain from trying to further persuade his wife, and realized that he recognized that her quiet but adamant refusal was final. That Mrs. Richmond's strength of character was already known to her husband was evident by the respect and resignation in his eyes.

At last, when all was ready, Lieutenant Edwards gave a sharp command. A soldier shoved Timothy and John forward to the front of the rows of convicts. Timothy reeled, but John managed to stop him from falling to the ground. Elizabeth saw his lips move, and then Timothy straightened a little. John moved slightly away, and once more his dark gaze swept over the watching crowd, not faltering as it passed over the two women.

The hours that followed were to sear Elizabeth's memory forever and made her a devout proponent of the abolition of the use of flogging as a punishment and deterrent for convicts. At one stage she remembered the thick, mottled scars on her father's back and understood as never before what he must have endured.

She decided that flogging had to be one of the most humiliating invasions of the body that could befall a prisoner. Surely for the majority of people the emotional damage inflicted by the lash must be even worse than the physical. And yet it was the physical that she found so horrifying that several times she felt she must lose her senses.

Only once did Captain Longman try to order the two women below. Elizabeth did not try to hide her scorn of him as they refused. Color rose on his lined cheeks, and he dropped his eyes before hurrying away.

Lieutenant Edwards did not approach them, but his chest seemed to stick out more prominently as he barked orders to his men.

Elizabeth gritted her teeth, suddenly realizing as one poor wretch stumbled away and he barked an order for another to take his turn that the lieutenant seemed to actually be enjoying his power over those men. Then another thought struck her.

Surely he could not think that watching his power over others would somehow heighten her regard for him!

Only once more did Elizabeth see John Martin look toward her. For one fleeting moment his dark gaze lingered on her before he stared woodenly away, his expression shuttered.

Timothy seemed in much worse shape than his tall, well-built companion. He seemed to be in a daze, and only his friend's strong arm around him kept him from falling. His clothes were heavily bloodstained and hanging in strips from him, his face swollen and smeared with blood from a cut on his forehead.

The other convicts were flogged first, and every time Timothy or John dared to look away the soldier guarding them cuffed them with the butt of his rifle. Obviously part of their punishment was to watch their fellow prisoners suffering.

And suffer they did.

Some men cried out from the first lash of the vicious thongs of leather. A few older, tougher men somehow managed to stifle their pain and received murmurs of approval from watching sailors, soldiers, and convicts. One older salt even called out, "You're a real Pebble, man," as one short, stockily built man, his harsh face lined, his hair streaked with gray, never uttered a murmur as his back became slowly criss-crossed with weals and trickles of blood.

Elizabeth glanced enquiringly at Dr. Richmond, who had stood between the two women after acknowledging their adamant refusals to go below.

"A 'Sandstone' is a man who is soft under the lash, a 'Pebble' is much harder and an 'Iron Man'. . ." He stopped abruptly as Elizabeth could not prevent the shudder that shook her.

When each trembling figure stumbled away, Elizabeth's mind numbly wondered what fifty lashes would be like.

Then Timothy was prodded forward.

Elizabeth sucked in a deep breath and looked swiftly at John. His expression did not change, but Elizabeth noted his lips had thinned to a straight line.

Her heart shrieked out to God, *Where are You? Why don't You stop this horror, this suffering?*__

Timothy stumbled. He was dragged upright and groaned loudly as his arms were bound around the mast. Then the remnants of the rags on his back were ripped away. He stiffened and suddenly sagged against the post.

A peculiar stillness fell over the watching convicts. Then a loud, mocking voice called out, "Where's your God now, Holy Joe?"

John's head whipped around, and he stared hard in the direction of the voice. He remained silent, but several indignant voices cursed the man until the soldiers barked out commands for silence.

The whip made its peculiar crackle. White marks appeared on the pale back. Ten more times it lashed down, turning the skin to a bright pink, then red as the skin was broken. Not once did Timothy cry out.

After the sergeant had called out the tenth stroke in his monotonous voice, Dr. Richmond's loud, angry voice cried out, "One moment, please."

Lieutenant Edwards moved swiftly to intercept him as he strode toward Timothy. "Dr. Richmond. . ."

The doctor interrupted him harshly. "It is my responsibility to determine if this man can stand any more punishment at this time."

"The law says you only should examine after fifty—"

"The law says many things, Lieutenant Edwards," interrupted the doctor loudly, "including that the health of these men is my responsibility. I also make out every one of my reports in at least duplicate!"

His voice held a definite threat on the last words. It was obvious his report on the lieutenant would already not be favorable. The two men eyed each other tensely, and then to Elizabeth's relief the officer moved back.

Unfortunately for Timothy, he gave a low groan and

straightened slightly as Dr. Richmond swiftly examined him. After a lengthy pause, the doctor hesitated and then nodded briefly to the grim-faced man holding the cat-o'-nine-tails.

"Sir. . .sir," Elizabeth protested in a low voice as he rejoined them. She stopped abruptly at the swift shake of the head the doctor gave her and the warning look in his eyes.

"I thought he was unconscious. If I stopped it now, it would only begin all over again at another time. Best to get it over with," he whispered softly in clipped words.

The next few strokes cut the skin in several more places until blood was trickling freely. Elizabeth closed her eyes tightly.

A loud, tormented voice with a slight accent rang out. "No more! Add the rest to my number!"

Every head swivelled toward John Martin. There was a sudden deathly silence. He shuffled forward a few paces toward Lieutenant Edwards, his chains ringing out loudly in the stillness.

For once the officer was disconcerted. He gaped at the man approaching him who was daring to show such friendship, such compassion. Lieutenant Edwards even fell back a step before collecting himself and looking a little frantically toward his sergeant. That worthy gentleman marched swiftly over to him, and whatever he said seemed to decide the matter.

Edwards backed farther away from the convict who towered over him both physically and mentally. He held a dainty handkerchief delicately to his nose. Suddenly he looked across the deck with narrowed eyes at Elizabeth. She stared directly back at him.

For a long moment he continued to hesitate. Then he glared up at the convict and suddenly screamed, "You'll not only have the rest of his cuts to your back but another ten for insolence, you dog!"

Elizabeth heard Dr. Richmond mutter softly under his breath. He started forward and assisted the soldier releasing the crumpled figure at the mast. Immediately it was obvious

Timothy could not walk. The doctor glared defiantly at Lieutenant Edwards and summoned two convicts to carry Timothy below.

As if in some dreadful dream, Elizabeth was aware of all that was happening with Timothy, but not once did she remove her eyes from John Martin. He shuffled forward to take his punishment, and she drew in one swift, quivering breath.

After a while, the sound of leather striking flesh and the sergeant's voice intoning the number of lashes blended together in a haze of pain. Her anguish for John was too deep for tears.

The doctor returned to examine the tall, once-strong figure at least twice, but each time reluctantly stepped aside. The dreadful flogging went on. Only vaguely was she aware that Mrs. Richmond moved and put an arm around her.

Then at last the dreadful ordeal was over. Once again the doctor helped release the prisoner. But John pushed away those who would help him and stumbled and wove his way toward the hatch. For the last few minutes, the convicts had been still and quiet. A sudden shout of approval roared forth.

Elizabeth made to move forward, but the arm supporting her tightened its grip. "No, no," Mrs. Richmond murmured sharply. "You must stay here. It will only increase that monster's hatred for the poor. . .poor. . ."

It was the stifled sob in her friend's voice that stopped Elizabeth. She straightened and turned to find that Mrs. Richmond was right. Lieutenant Edwards was watching her avidly. Somehow she stifled the sobs that were struggling to take over her trembling body. She raised her head and stared back at him steadily, feeling nothing when it was he who looked away first.

Elizabeth stared dazedly at the sergeant who was waiting to speak to his commanding officer. Then her gaze wandered to the scourger who was leaning heavily against the ship's rail. They were both drenched in sweat. The midday sun was extremely hot. Everyone on deck was feeling its effects, especially the convicts forced to stand still. Surely the horror must stop soon.

As she stared around, gradually her dazed mind became aware that the captain and his officers were hurrying away. Even as she watched, the ship's crew started to disperse. Suddenly she realized the rolling of the ship had increased. Even as she swung around to look seaward, the deck beneath their feet heaved up so sharply both women were almost flung off their feet.

"Man the topsail. Get those sails in. Get those convicts below deck."

Captain Longman's voice roared out moments before the ship plunged down. There were loud cries of fright from both convicts and soldiers. Several were flung to the deck.

A low bank of dark clouds rolled toward them across the white-flecked ocean. The ship rose up on the crest of another huge wave. Several strong gusts of wind struck the ship, and then it plunged down again. Elizabeth and Mrs. Richmond hung on grimly to the rail and each other.

Suddenly there was a chorus of shouted commands. Captain Longman's voice roared again. "Clear that deck! Get those men below!"

Sailors had sprung into action everywhere. Many were climbing the riggings to furl the sails. The soldiers barely glanced toward their two officers before beginning to herd their charges below deck.

Elizabeth and Mrs. Richmond carefully made their way down the gangway. At the entrances to their cabins, they paused, looked at each other, and with one accord made their way farther along to the cabin that had been used several times now as a sick bay. Even as they reached it they could hear Dr. Richmond's voice snapping out instructions.

Dr. Richmond glanced up briefly from the still body of Timothy and barked, "About time! Here, one of you hold this arm." His wife moved swiftly forward as he added angrily, "How could I have missed that broken arm and shoulder?"

Elizabeth's gaze swept swiftly around the cabin. Relief filled her when she saw the large body face down in the other bunk.

Mrs. Richmond nodded toward John. "Do what you can for him, my dear."

Fearfully she started to wash the blood away from his torn back, wincing as a muffled groan was wrenched from him, wishing fervently that he was unconscious like his friend.

The squall struck in full force. Grimly they fought to care for their charges as the ship pitched and rolled. Once Elizabeth was almost flung across the room. A strong arm reached out and grabbed her. Dark eyes blazed at her for one brief moment before John let her go and closed his eyes again.

She was more careful after that, and it took a long time to cleanse his wounds. The movement of the ship made even standing upright very difficult.

Only once more did he open his eyes. In a soft voice filled with wonder he croaked out, "You shouldn't be doing this. You shouldn't have even been there."

She closed her eyes briefly and then stared earnestly at him. "Yes, I should," she whispered back in a choked voice. "I'm not sure if it did or not, but we hoped that our being there would. . .would help."

"Yes, it helped."

He didn't say anything more for a long time, and then she heard him murmur, his voice filled with wonder, "You. . .you didn't leave. You stayed and. . .and. . ."

Elizabeth saw a faint smile soften his whole face. Then to her relief the effect of the small dose of laudanum Dr. Richmond had given him from his precious supply took effect, and he even dozed off.

During the rest of that day and into the dark hours of the night, Mrs. Richmond showed she was no stranger to sickrooms as she bossed Elizabeth around. The two women spent the night in the cabin while the ship tossed and rolled its way through the storm. Dr. Richmond had many other patients from the riot as well as the storm, and when he returned late that evening, his concerned wife sternly insisted the red-eyed, exhausted man try to get some sleep.

"Go on, my dear," she urged him, "I'd be surprised if both these men escape having a fever the morrow, and who knows what other injuries you'll have to attend before the sea calms. The last thing we need is a sick doctor."

In the end he was forced to acknowledge she was right. After sternly admonishing the women to call him if they needed him, he left them to watch over the two men.

"Although I've been very thankful there have been no female convicts on board this ship, another woman's hand would have been welcome this night," Mrs. Richmond said grimly after he had gone.

The ship tossed and reeled its way through the dark night, but when dawn arrived the skies were still black, although the wind and the rain had eased some of their fury.

To both women's dismay, Timothy had not regained consciousness. John had spent a very restless night, and was undoubtedly starting a fever. After she straightened from feeling his forehead and observing his flushed cheeks, Mrs. Richmond sighed. "Well, it's as I thought. We'll have a very busy day ahead of us with these two," she said grimly.

Turning to Elizabeth she said in a voice that defied any argument, "Go at once and have a rest, change those clothes, and have something to eat. Then I'll take my turn as soon as my husband returns."

Elizabeth numbly did as she was told, even dozing briefly before coming awake with a start and rushing back to the makeshift hospital room.

Dr. Richmond was there alone. He surveyed her for a moment, and then said briefly, "My wife is resting." He nodded toward Timothy. "He has stirred several times and is now in a natural sleep. The other one. . ."

He paused and shook his head wearily. "He never has fully recovered from his congestion of the lungs, and now infection of his back has set in as well."

Something had changed in Elizabeth during those horrifying events the previous day. Calmly she moved forward and felt John's burning forehead. He opened dazed eyes, stared at her with some undefinable expression, and turned his head away.

She steadily met the doctor's weary eyes. "Tell me what I must do, Dr. Richmond."

After rapping out instructions, he hurried away. Mrs. Richmond returned a little later and said grimly, "I've managed to convince Dr. Richmond to let me accompany him to check on the other convicts. There is far too much for him to do alone, and he doesn't completely trust the convicts, or soldiers for that matter, to tend to the injured properly."

With that, she too disappeared. Elizabeth took a deep breath and returned to persuading John to swallow more fluids. A little later with considerable relief, she welcomed the wide-eyed cabin boy, who shyly informed her he had been sent to help.

They were once again bathing the weeping wounds on John's poor back when a grim-faced Sergeant Hobbs flung the door open.

Elizabeth sprang defensively to her feet. Before she could speak, the sergeant dismissed the cabin boy with a nod. As he scurried away, Sergeant Hobbs barked, "How are they, ma'am?"

She had been gritting her teeth, trying to stop the tears of outrage and grief at the pain she had just been forced to give John, and at the sergeant's words, she opened her mouth to furiously denounce him, Lieutenant Edwards, and every soldier on board. But he had moved to peer from one bunk to the other, and she read genuine concern in his exhausted, weathered face.

He gestured impatiently. "Is Hardy going to be all right? Doctor said he's broken some bones."

"See for yourself," she said curtly. "He only regained consciousness very briefly during the night and has not stirred since."

Sergeant Hobbs moved closer to examine the small man. "I told him he was hurt bad," he muttered angrily and then sighed. "Doubt if he felt anything after that first coupla strokes."

There was no need for Elizabeth to ask whom he meant. After a brief moment, she said feelingly, "He will when he wakes."

"He won't be as bad as he woulda been if this other fool here had not. . ."

The harsh voice stopped abruptly. He was still scowling as he turned and advanced toward John. Elizabeth drew in a quick breath. John was watching them.

Sergeant Hobbs stared at him silently. Then he shook his head slowly and said in a wondering voice, "Why would a murderin' scum like they say you are do a thing like that!"

Elizabeth looked at the sergeant in some surprise, first at the astonishment in his voice and then at the sudden realization that she had not felt any real surprise at all that John Martin was capable of acting in such a way. She had seen before the genuine affection he had for Timothy. Besides, she had already once seen him risk his own life in the dark water of the Thames.

Sergeant Hobbs muttered angrily, "And despite what Lieutenant Edwards said, several of my men insist you were trying to stop the riot, not start it, and even helped prevent us from being injured by the rest of them scum."

"Timothy tried to stop them too." John's voice was weak, but still angry. He stirred and then caught his breath as pain clawed him. "They. . .they are not all scum, just very frightened, angry men deprived of their freedom in that hole."

He scowled at the sergeant and then glanced quickly at Elizabeth. "Are you sure Timothy's going to be all right? I knew he had been trampled, but I couldn't get to him quickly enough."

Elizabeth took a moment to swallow the sudden lump in her throat. This was the first time since those moments the night before that he had spoken to her.

"Besides his broken arm and shoulder, Timothy is all right. Dr. Richmond has assured us that the bump on his head does not seem too severe."

Relief flickered on John's face. He relaxed and closed his eyes. The sergeant had been watching them both. He suddenly scowled and put out a large hand toward John. Elizabeth moved swiftly forward, only to stop as the rough soldier's hand gently touched the wide forehead.

"He's burnin' up with fever," he exclaimed.

"Yes." She took a deep breath. "Dr. Richmond thinks it's a combination of some return of his previous lung trouble, shock, infection on his. . .his back, and the general debilitation all the convicts are suffering from."

John's eyes flew open again. He stared warily back at the sergeant. That gentleman turned slowly and studied her accusing face. She held his gaze steadily.

Suddenly he straightened and took a deep breath. "Well, at least I can now do somethin' about some of it." He hesitated and then said formally, "Until Lieutenant Edwards recovers, I am taking over his responsibilities."

"Lieutenant Edwards is ill?"

The man suddenly grinned at her, and Elizabeth was startled at the way it changed him from a stern soldier to an approachable man.

"Well," he drawled, "if bein' out like a light since banging his head falling down the gangway in his hurry to get down from topside when the storm started is ill, he's ill."

"Does Dr. Richmond know?"

To Elizabeth's utter amazement, the man winked at her. "Dr. Richmond has been run off his feet like, Miss Waverley, and we didn't like to bother him last night, like. That is," he added hurriedly, but still with a glint in his eyes, "not until we'd obeyed orders, like, and made sure all the convicts were safely locked away below deck. Besides, no one really knew the lieutenant was missing for a very long time. It's very dark in them passageways with no lights allowed because of the storm and all.

"Then when I did stumble over him. . .well. . .had no time with the storm and all to find the good doctor last night, you might say, Miss. Only had time to dump. . .er put the lieutenant on his bed, like." He shrugged carelessly. "No one seems to know how long he laid there in the passageway before anyone noticed 'im, neither."

Elizabeth continued to stare at him, not sure whether to laugh or feel sorry for a man who had so dreadfully lost the loyalty and respect of his men. Then she silently wondered why the doctor had not mentioned the accident.

Suddenly the man in front of her stiffened as though remembering to whom he was speaking. All amusement disappeared, and he briefly saluted her and marched toward the door. There he turned.

"No sayin' how long lieutenant'll be out of action, and I have me own as well as his duties. I'll send you what help I can," he finished abruptly, hesitated a moment, and then added warningly, "only I don't know nothin' about it at all later on, if you understand me, Miss." Then he was gone.

six

Lieutenant Edwards kept to his cabin. Only once did Dr. Richmond volunteer any information about him. "His head's hard enough to mend without any problems," he growled. "It'll ache for a good while, though."

Unfortunately he was not as optimistic about Timothy's recovery, and the first few days shook his head over the still semi-conscious man.

To their relief, John recovered quite rapidly from his fever, and his back started to slowly dry up. The dreadful wounds began to heal over, but Elizabeth knew he would carry the scars the rest of his life.

But as the days passed, Elizabeth privately worried about him. "Sometimes there's such a dreadful look in his eyes," she whispered to her friend. "He stares into the distance so and. . .I. . .I'm so afraid. . ."

Mrs. Richmond nodded grimly. "My husband has told me many times that flogging can sometimes do something to a man's spirit that will take years to heal, if ever." After a moment she added quietly, "We must just continue to give him and Mr. Hardy all the care we can as well as pray for healing of their minds and hearts."

When John was well enough to be returned below deck, they appealed to the sergeant to permit John to stay and help with Timothy. That tough but compassionate soldier was more than willing to allow it.

The sergeant was already starting to improve the conditions among the convicts, following without any demur the doctor's suggestions. They were allowed on deck more often for various reasons, including extra work that was allocated to them to alleviate the boredom.

Elizabeth was surprised how quickly most of those who had been flogged recovered, and one day she earnestly complimented the sergeant.

His rugged features relaxed into a pleased smile and then he murmured, "Just followed the surgeon's instructions, Miss Waverley, ma'am. Extra rations of rum were used on the backs to clean 'em and not poured down their mouths."

She smiled gently at him. "It certainly seemed to stop the infection on our patients." Hesitantly she said, "And your lieutenant is improving, so I am told?"

The man's face darkened. "Not well enough to be issuing orders yet. On other ships I've been on it has been the captain who has been responsible for discipline and order. Even our officers have to obey the captain. If it had been so here. . ."

He paused and then continued gruffly. "Captain Longman has, and not before time, if you'll pardon me, ma'am, insisted to 'im that 'e is in charge and I am following his orders and. . .and so far Lieutenant Edwards 'as not summoned me to 'is cabin."

That rather pleasant state of affairs continued as the ship plowed across the empty ocean and ever closer to their destination. Mrs. Richmond gradually relaxed her vigil over her charge, seemingly willing to leave Elizabeth alone at times with the two convicts.

To everyone's relief, Timothy gradually regained his senses. He obediently took the nourishment offered to him, would smile his sweet smile, and then usually fell asleep again.

The atmosphere between Elizabeth and John after that first night became very tense. He was silent, not volunteering any conversation, and when forced to speak to her did so in sharp monosyllables. She had hoped they would quickly regain the easy rapport that had grown between them during his last confinement to this cabin, but she found that his continued silences began to agitate her more and more. Despite her anguish for what he had been through, she started to feel not only frustrated and a little angry, but also hurt that he persisted in practically ignoring her.

There was little she could do or say while under Mrs. Richmond's eagle eye, but one day she was sitting quietly reading when that lady was absent, and to her surprise and delight, John asked quietly, "Does that happen to be a Bible you're reading, Miss Waverley?"

She looked up and answered, "Why yes, of course." She smiled gently at him and added, "But I thought I was Elizabeth, not that cold 'Miss Waverley' anymore."

He stared into her eyes for a long moment. Briefly she saw a flash of pain before he looked down again at the large, rather battered book in her hands. There was a long pause, and she found her heart lifting in prayer for him. She hesitated, wondering what he would say if she offered to lend the Bible to him, or to read out loud.

While she was wondering what to do, he suddenly looked directly at her. For one more brief moment she saw a crack in the expressionless face and cold gaze that had been on his face since the flogging. There was such a look of longing, of vulnerability, that she held her breath, but then he turned his head sharply away to center his gaze once again on the still form of his friend.

"Would you like to borrow my Bible, John?" she asked quickly.

He was still for a moment, and then he turned very slowly and looked at her again. "No, thank you. I have been sharing the small one Timothy has managed to hang onto." He paused and then added grimly, "That is if it has not been stolen again while we've been here."

Something thrilled inside her that at last he was talking to her. "Someone stole his Bible?" she asked a little breathlessly. "Who would ever steal a Bible?"

His lips twisted in a grimace, and he gave a harsh laugh. "It was taken when I was sick. We did get it back, minus a few pages used to roll their filthy tobacco in."

Elizabeth refrained from asking how he had managed to find it. "It's hard to understand how anyone could steal a

Bible," she said quietly, "or to so misuse it."

She hated the harsh sound that he gave before he sneered, "All except a handful of those men below deck would steal anything if they thought they needed it, Miss Waverley."

"Oh, please," she burst out, "do call me Elizabeth like you used to."

His expression hardened. "That proved to be very foolish, Miss Waverley," he said in cold tones.

Tears sprang to her eyes, and she angrily dashed them away. "You do blame me for the severity of your. . .your punishment, but not anywhere near as much as I blame myself!"

He stood up so quickly the small chair he had been sitting on fell over. "Blame you! No, no," he said in a choked voice. "How could I blame you for. . .for being there, for staying! But I hated for you to be touched by any of that ghastly business, to be there to see me. . .see me. . .but you were so brave, so. . ."

He paused, swallowed, and added quickly, "I can assure you some of the old lags muttered that the scourger's arm was surprisingly weaker than it usually was. They gave you two women the credit." He stopped abruptly and turned away.

Elizabeth stood and went to him. It was as though she had no control over her feet or the hands that reached out to gently touch his clenched ones. "Oh, John, but you and Timothy paid in part for my foolishness in allowing. . .in letting that. . . that man think that I. . ."

She stumbled to a halt, tears running freely down her cheeks, and she lowered her head, hoping to hide them.

His hands turned and convulsively clutched her small, dainty ones. Then he placed a firm finger under her chin and raised her face and wiped at her wet cheeks so gently with the back of his hand that the tears flowed even faster and a small sob escaped.

Suddenly he let go of her hands only to wrap his arms gently around her until she was cradled against his strong body. Her own hands came up to circle his body, but as she touched him he winced, and she let her hands fall helplessly beside her and just leaned all her weight onto him.

Never before had she felt such a feeling of safety. . .of security, but suddenly he wrenched away from her and turned his back.

His rigid shoulders heaved once. Then he spat out a stream of furious words in a foreign language.

With a trembling hand, Elizabeth wiped her cheeks. She managed to give a small laugh, and it was one of the most difficult things she had ever done. "I'm afraid I don't speak any Spanish, my dear John. You will have to tell me all that again in English."

Neither of them moved. Then Elizabeth wrapped her arms around her waist. He sensed her slight movement and turned slowly toward her. For a long time he stared at her, and she bravely returned his look.

"I should not have touched you, Miss Waverley." His face had lost its hectic flush and was deathly pale. He gave her a slight, formal bow and said in the expressionless voice she hated, "Please accept my sincere apologies."

Elizabeth just stared at him. A violent shiver swept through her.

That seemed to shake him more than any words could. "Oh, my dear, don't you see, I am a man condemned to living imprisonment for the rest of my life!" The words burst from him in a torrent. "Someone so. . .so pure as you cannot have anything to do with such as I. Last time. . .last time being deprived of your brightness made the darkness seem even darker. . .more difficult."

Relief and sadness in equal measure swept through Elizabeth. "I am not foolish enough to think we can be anything more than friends, sir." Even as the words left her lips she knew that some deep, inner part of her refused to believe them.

"We should not even be friends!"

Anger touched her. "No one tells me whom I can be friends with. Friendship just. . .just happens."

"Not if the 'friends' cannot see each other."

"True friendship withstands time and distance."

He was silent, then whispered, "But not a lifetime of imprisonment."

She too was quiet for a long moment. "Perhaps that is why I so much want to try and prove your innocence, John Martin."

Such a look of longing filled his face that she had to bite her lip to stop crying out. Instead, she added rapidly, "I want you to finish telling me your story."

"But you cannot befriend a convict!"

"I already have." Her spirit lightened. His voice had held less conviction, and she smiled faintly at him. "In fact I believe I have now befriended perhaps three—no. . ." She put her head on one side, "I considered one of the convicts assigned to my father my friend, so I guess that makes four."

She laughed outright at his astonished face. "I am a currency lass, remember?" She chuckled again at the bewilderment in his face. "You haven't heard that expression before? Those of us born in Australia are called currency lads and lassies as opposed to people born in England called British Sterling."

She became serious again. "It's different from England—especially out west where we have to rely so much on each other."

John stared at her, and their eyes studied each other carefully. Suddenly she did not know what to say. Instead of urging him again to tell her about himself, she sat staring down at her clenched hands. There had been a gleam in his eyes that had not been there before, and she bit her lip, wondering if perhaps he would prefer a woman who was not as bold, as willing to be friendly.

"Perhaps I should tell you a little more about myself," she blurted out at last.

He hesitated and then nodded. So she told him briefly about growing up on a small farm and then the upheaval of moving farther west. "Father took up land that he could graze thousands of sheep on. He did very well," she said simply. "Then my mother died, and it was as though a light inside him had been turned off. He gradually withdrew, even from me."

Her voice wobbled a little, but she smiled. "I never doubted he loved me, even when he insisted on sending me to England to learn how to be a lady, as he put it." She pulled a face. "I tried very hard there, but I seemed not to have much in common with the girls in England. Every time I wrote, I begged Father to let me come home but he always put me off."

She fell silent, and at last he said softly, "You mentioned convicts assigned to your father when you moved. There has been talk among the men about the possibility of being assigned. No one seemed too sure what being assigned means except they worry about it a great deal.

"One man told some of us about an old acquaintance of his, one of the Tolpuddle men transported for trade union activity last year. He was assigned to a magistrate on the Hunter River. James Brine was forced to dig postholes, even though he had bare feet that were so cut and sore that he could not put them to the spade. There were other stories. . ." He stopped and then asked slowly, "Does your father still have some working for him?"

"Since I've been in England, I do not know. He has never mentioned them in his letters to me," she answered quietly. "A man called Adam Stevens was assigned to him before I left. He is serving a ten-year sentence for fraud. Anyone assigned to my father is treated very well if they work hard and do the right thing by him," she said with a proud tilt to her head.

"How does the system work?"

"In 1831 I believe there were 13,400 assigned convicts, but for some time now there has been a move to stop the practice," she continued rapidly. "From what I understand, anyone who wants a convict to work for them has to apply to the government. I remember once my father had to pay his convicts ten pounds a year, but Governor Darling changed that not long before I went to England. Now the master has only to issue essentials like blankets and clothes instead.

"There are all kinds of laws to try and protect convicts and the men who have them but. . .but I heard my father say there are good and bad men among convicts and masters alike who abuse the whole system."

Still staring intently at her, John nodded thoughtfully. "My grandfather's farm in Spain had sheep—many sheep!"

"In his last short letter that arrived a few months ago, my father told me he was considering buying more sheep and moving even farther west."

They stared at each other. Her heart beating faster, Elizabeth looked away first.

After a moment she said a little breathlessly, "You. . .you worked on your father, Lord. . .Lord Farnley's estate also?"

"Yes." His voice was thick, more heavily accented.

She dared to glance quickly at him. Her eyes lingered on his pale, tense face as he went on to tell her about the long hours he had worked with Lord Farnley's gamekeeper.

"He was a good man, poor Jock Macallister, a good man. His granddaughter was very beautiful, and he had a hard job keeping an eye on her, he did."

Elizabeth's eyes narrowed.

He scowled and added, "He was right to. Why, even Lord Farnley's heir, Sir Percival, cast his eyes her way."

"Sir Percival?"

"Yes," he said briefly. "I did not like him. His father was my. . .Lord Farnley's only brother. I still sometimes wonder if—" He stopped abruptly, and Elizabeth saw his hands move convulsively.

"He would be your cousin then, John."

At her soft words, a dark look filled his face. "Oh, yes, treacherous Percival Farnley is my cousin."

He looked into the distance, and Elizabeth waited quietly, hoping he would continue. Her patience was rewarded when he uttered short, harsh words. "I first met him one day in the woods near Jock's cottage. He was with Jenny. A very haughty, angry young man I thought him." He gave a mirthless laugh. "He called me an insolent rogue when I offered to escort Jenny home."

"Jenny?"

John glanced at her sharply. "Jock's granddaughter. I didn't at all like the attention he was giving her, and neither would have her grandfather. Fortunately Beth arrived, and she walked back with us both. For some reason Jenny was very upset, and I was glad to let Beth talk to her."

Elizabeth clenched her hands and waited. She was not sure if he had guessed she had heard what he had told Timothy all those weeks ago, and she was not at all sure she wanted him to tell her any more about the woman he had called out for so many times when he had been out of his senses.

"Beth. . ." John took a deep breath, "Beth was the daughter of my. . .Lord Farnley's last wife. She was very beautiful, and everyone told me that he had always favored her more than Kate."

Another woman! Elizabeth was not sure she wanted to know about any more women in his life. A little sharply she asked, "Who is Kate?"

"Kate is my. . .my half sister. She is only a couple years younger than me. Apparently my father quickly found someone else to marry when he returned after the war with the French. Then when she died some years later, he married Beth's mother."

He paused for a while, and Elizabeth could only look at him sadly and be thankful for the wonderful love that had always existed between her own mother and father.

"Beth is very beautiful, has such incredibly blue eyes. Even more than a beautiful face, she has such a caring heart—or that was what I thought for a long time."

Elizabeth looked up. His voice had thickened.

"I was with her when Jock was killed."

She could not bear the pain and hurt in his voice and said

swiftly, "I heard you tell Timothy about her." What she really wanted to know was whether he loved Beth.

He stared at her, and a tinge of color crept up his high cheekbones. She looked down at the hands in her lap and realized they were tearing at her handkerchief.

"I also heard you tell him you found Jock Macallister," she blurted out.

His gaze darkened. Then he closed his eyes as though trying to block out the ghastly memories.

"He had been stabbed," he said shortly. "The knife was still in him. Instinctively I tried to remove it, but while I was trying to pull it out, Percival arrived with his servants. He accused me loudly and hauled me off to the magistrate."

The stark words ceased. Elizabeth knew there must be more, much more. She held her breath, waiting for him to continue, but he remained silent.

A soft voice beside them asked, "Did you hear him tell me Beth could have proved he was with her, but the fool was too honorable to mention her until it was too late?"

They turned to see Timothy watching them both. Elizabeth exclaimed, "Why sir, you are awake and looking so much better too!"

"Probably well enough to be returned to our other fancy quarters," Timothy said with a wry smile.

"Oh, I can't bear the thought of you down in that dreadful place," cried Elizabeth. "Mrs. Richmond won't let me go down there, but she has told me how dark and crowded and odorous it is."

Timothy gave a slight shrug and then winced. Although his back was nowhere near as bad as John's, any unwary movement pulled on the scars starting to form. "I think you should tell Elizabeth all you can about what happened if she still is determined to help you, John."

John was silent, and Elizabeth's heart sank, wishing that Timothy had not spoken and broken the atmosphere between them.

Then, to her relief, John said shortly, "There's not much more to tell."

Timothy stared at him. "What about Beth's part?" he said indignantly at last. "Don't you still believe she should have vouched for you, spoken up at your trial?"

John shook his head.

Elizabeth looked from one grim face to the other. She wondered even more about this Beth. How could any woman turn her back when she might have saved an innocent man from the gallows?

John scowled at Timothy. "I really don't see much point in talking any more about it. I've been sentenced. I'm here. I'll be here for the rest of my miserable life, and that may not be too long if the events of a few days ago are repeated."

Elizabeth sprang to her feet. "That's a terrible thing to say! You can't give up!"

That cold, distant expression she hated so much, even feared, was back on John's face. "I don't see that it is really any of your business, Miss Waverley."

Elizabeth began to tremble. Then she felt a spark of anger. "You're right, Mr. Martin, your affairs are certainly none of my business," she snapped, "but I do believe a great wrong has been done to you. Any person with an ounce of decency or compassion in them would seek to right that wrong." With a swish of her long full gown she rose, and a moment later was gone.

John stood very still. For a moment the sharp agony in his heart rivaled the lash of the cat-o'-nine-tails.

"That was not very well done, my friend," Timothy's quiet voice said behind him. "She is a good woman and considers you her friend."

"And that's the very reason I had to speak to her like that," John said in a low, passion-filled voice. "There is no future in it. . .a beautiful young woman like her getting too fond. . .too friendly with a convict. It could ruin her whole life. You saw yourself how that man treated her."

"Since you started praying with me, I hoped you might have wondered like I have if God's hand is not in all of this." Timothy's voice was very quiet. "How many times do you think a God-fearing, good woman like Elizabeth Waverley would just happen to be on any convict ship, let alone this particular one where a man like yourself was being sent to pay for a crime he has not committed?"

John stared at him, an arrested look on his face. "God's hand? You really think. . ." He suddenly shook his head sharply. "No. I might now believe that God loved me enough to send the Christ to save me from hell. But why would God trouble Himself more than that for someone like me? You perhaps, a good person who has long ago committed his life to Christ, but not me."

"And that same person could no doubt have died under the lash without a tall, strong man to take his stripes on himself. How do I thank you for that? You took my place and. . ."

Timothy stopped and drew in a sharp breath.

"Stripes," he murmured after a pause. "Jesus took our stripes. He was whipped, scourged, but it was for sin—oh, not His own, for yours and mine. With His stripes we are healed," he finished with a smile.

John glared at him. "What's this about stripes? You told me about Him being crucified but not about a. . .a flogging."

"Didn't I? It was all part and parcel of the crucifixion scene, I guess." Timothy relaxed back on his pillows. "It was the Roman soldiers who did it, but it was like this. . ."

seven

"Congratulations, Captain. Dr. Richmond has told me that your ship has made very good time."

Captain Longman acknowledged Elizabeth's civil words with a slight bow. "Just so, Miss Waverley, just so. It is only one hundred and twenty days since we left England," he boasted with a beaming smile. "The winds have on the whole been very favorable to us, especially this last part of our journey. We will be entering the heads of Port Jackson early tomorrow."

Elizabeth privately thought that the winds since leaving the fledgling colony at Fremantle on the western shores of Australia could have been a little kinder to them. It had blown a gale for days, certainly sending the *Royal Lady* flying over the water, but not giving its weary passengers a very pleasant time as it pitched and tossed. Still, it was wonderful to be close to the end of this harrowing journey.

"You must be very excited at the thought of soon seeing your father, Miss Waverley," said a voice near her elbow.

On the surface the words were pleasant, all that was polite, but Elizabeth stiffened slightly. She turned and saw the slight sneer on Lieutenant Cecil Edwards' face. Not once since he had at last left his cabin and rejoined their company had a word been said between them about the dreadful consequences of the convicts' poor treatment and the riot, but Elizabeth knew that she had made an enemy.

To everyone's relief, the lieutenant had not tried to assert himself above the captain again. Elizabeth had several times secretly wondered if that was more because of something Dr. Richmond may have said to him than the fact that the flogging incident or his accident may have changed him. But whatever the cause, except for a couple minor skirmishes among a few convicts, there had been no other incidents to mar the rest of the journey.

"Of course, Lieutenant Edwards," she said briefly. She caught Mrs. Richmond's watchful eye and added reluctantly, "Are you all packed, sir?"

He nodded and then to her relief turned away as Dr. Richmond hurried into the dining room.

"There you are, sir," his wife said severely. "We are all waiting upon you to commence our last dinner together."

As the doctor apologized, Elizabeth saw the comfortable smile the two exchanged, and a pang raced through her. How pleasant it would be to have a marriage where each understood the other so well.

It was a festive evening. Not even the occasional sneering comments by the lieutenant could dampen the excitement that surrounded them at the thought that their long journey would conclude the very next day.

Elizabeth's own excitement was tempered by two things. One was how her father would welcome her, and the other the continual nagging concern she had for John and Timothy.

She had been thrilled when Dr. Richmond had managed to have John assigned to looking after the women's needs. This had often included cleaning out their cabins, and several times she had managed to spend some time with him to coax him to relax his cold, withdrawn manner toward her.

Then one day he had looked at her and said hurriedly, "Timothy said you would want to know that I now believe that Jesus has forgiven me. I'm. . .I'm a believer."

She had stiffened, but before she could comment he had hurried away. There had been a noticeable softening in his whole demeanor, a light in his eyes that had dispelled the pain. She was very happy for him, but she had thought the change in him was because his feelings for her had been growing even as hers were for him.

The two men had succeeded in gathering a few of their

fellow convicts together for times of prayer and Bible reading. When trying to read her Bible and praying by herself in her cabin, she envied their fellowship, and a strange feeling of loneliness came over her at times, only dispelled when she saw John for precious few moments.

She had tried not to think of the horrible possibility of never seeing him again after they left the ship. She had determined shortly after the riot to petition her father to try to acquire both Timothy and John as assigned convicts, not that she'd mentioned the idea to Mrs. Richmond. She was sure the lady would be horrified.

But that last evening on board the *Royal Lady,* Elizabeth quietly asked Mrs. Richmond, "Do you know what happens to the convicts when we anchor in Sydney Cove tomorrow?"

Her friend looked at her for a moment and then replied as softly, "They have already been put in chains, ready to be marched ashore as soon as the appropriate government officials come aboard and do what they have to."

At the distressed sound Elizabeth made, her lips tightened. "You would be best to put all that has happened on this ship behind you, Elizabeth. Surely you always knew that any friendship with any of them was useless, quite useless, especially as your father. . ."

Elizabeth looked up quickly. "You know about his. . ." She paused, not sure whether to put her question into words, but her friend was nodding.

"You forget that your mother and I became very good friends. She told me that your father is an emancipist." She hesitated for a moment and then added gently, "And my husband and I both know that he never mentions those early years of his life here, unlike other prominent men who have served their time and seem to be proud of the fact they are emancipists."

"He has always been very busy establishing his property and putting its interests and his family first," Elizabeth said proudly.

"And that he has done very well, indeed," Mrs. Richmond added hastily. "But you would be advised to remember that except for the necessity of having assigned convicts to work for him because good servants and workmen are difficult to persuade to go out into the bush, he has never had anything to do with the current politics—even the current strong move to abolish the transportation system altogether."

Elizabeth suddenly noticed that Lieutenant Edwards was watching them with considerable interest from across the room and hoped he had not heard their softly spoken words. For a fleeting moment a very unpleasant expression flickered across his face, but it was gone so quickly she thought she must have been mistaken. She watched his handsome face change completely as he suddenly smiled at something the captain was saying, and yet something made her feel very uneasy.

Oh, it would be good to go ashore the next day away from this ship, its horrible memories, and that man. If only she could be certain of John's well-being. And Timothy's also, she reminded herself quickly. But she knew that the welfare of the tall, dark man with the unforgettable smile was what burdened her heart the most.

After dinner that evening, Elizabeth was too excited to retire early and went for one last moonlit walk along the deck. A couple times during the afternoon they had seen a faint smudge on the horizon to the west and known they were drawing close to land as the southerly winds drove them up the coast of New South Wales. Now nothing could be seen except where the bright moonlight turned the dark waters to silver.

"Good evenin', Miss Waverley."

Startled, she spun around and then relaxed. "And a good evening it is, Sergeant Hobbs." She and the sergeant had become quite good friends away from Lieutenant Edwards' ever-watchful eyes, and now she asked, "Do you think your wife may be at the wharf tomorrow to welcome you back, sir?"

"Oh, no, Miss, she knows better than that," he said cheerfully. "I'll be too busy tomorrow handing over our charges, and she wouldn't be able to be away so long from the children anyway."

Elizabeth was silent for a long moment. Quietly they shared the stillness of the night as the ship carried them ever closer to home. There wasn't even the murmur of a human voice, only the winds in the sails and the slap of the waves against the hull.

At last, in a low voice she asked, "What. . .what happens to the convicts tomorrow, sir?"

He stared at her for a moment and then said, "Well, very soon after the ship's tied up nice and tight, I reckon it'll be swarming with officials and government men checking documents and whatnot. Then. . ." He paused before adding slowly, "After all the passengers have gone ashore, I reckon we'll probably march those poor men below to wherever they have to go. Then in the next day or so there'll undoubtedly be a reckoning for their behavior, especially. . ." The sergeant stopped abruptly.

For a moment Elizabeth was frozen in horror. Then she said rapidly, "But surely enough punishment has already been meted out for. . .for anything that has happened on the journey."

Sergeant Hobbs hesitated and then said heavily, "Lieutenant Edwards will put in his report. It will depend. . ." Once again he stopped, looked at her for a moment, and then said hurriedly, "Miss Waverley, I am afraid for the two men you cared for after the floggin's, especially John Martin. Ever since we left England, Lieutenant Edwards has shown an uncommon interest in the man."

A cold chill swept through Elizabeth.

"Lieutenant Edwards refuses to listen to our assurances and. . .and seems to have taken a set on him," he added hurriedly in a low voice. "I. . .I thought you should know, like, but please don't say that I said anythin', if you please. It's just that some offenses are hangin' matters."

Before Elizabeth could speak, he gave a hasty bow and moved quickly away.

Elizabeth turned back to stare blindly out across the dark ocean. Oh, she knew only too well how her compassion for the two convicts had drawn Lieutenant Edwards' attention to them. But what else could he be planning that so concerned Sergeant Hobbs?

Sudden resolve tightened her lips and made her raise her chin. Let the lieutenant put in his report. She would have something to report herself! Nothing more would happen to John if it lay in her power, no matter what her father might say to her for involving herself in convicts' affairs.

The next day she was on deck early with Dr. Richmond and his wife to watch the ship enter the heads of Port Jackson and sail slowly up the beautiful harbor. As they passed the small sandy inlets, cliffs, and heavily timbered shoreline, she was amazed to see how many more fine buildings had been built among the trees during the years she had been in England.

Determined not to miss a moment, Elizabeth stayed on deck until the ship at last docked. The usual flotilla of small boats met them with many a coarse joke and message called across the water. As she had many times before, she wondered how those unfortunate people on that first fleet of eight ships had felt that hot January day in 1788 as they had at last unloaded here. Their journey had taken eight long months from Portsmouth.

She felt a touch of sadness that her father would not be there to meet her. All the arrangements had been made to travel with the Richmonds to her home beyond the Blue Mountains. So, as they at long last walked on unsteady sea legs along the wharf, it was with quite a shock that she suddenly saw a familiar face from home.

With a startled cry, Elizabeth lifted the front of her long skirt and rushed forward through the crowd. "Adam! Oh, Adam, is it really you?"

The tall, handsome man, dressed more neatly in his city clothes than she had ever seen him, turned and stared at her. A puzzled expression filled his eyes. Then recognition flashed across his handsome face. For a moment he stared as though he could not believe what he saw, and then he moved gladly forward.

Impulsively she thrust her hands out. As he reached to clasp them, a myriad of emotions chased across his face.

"Elizabeth! Oh, I'm sorry, I mean Miss Waverley. How did you get here so swiftly?" He let her hands go and then looked at Dr. Richmond and his wife as they joined them. "Dr. Richmond, Mrs. Richmond!"

"So swiftly?" Her merry laugh rang out. "Why, it seemed such a long, long journey." She looked eagerly around. "Oh, Adam, is my father here too? How is he? What wonderful chance has brought you to Sydney and to this ship?" Elizabeth continued to peer around at the bustling crowd, still searching for her father.

With another happy, excited laugh Elizabeth swung back to him again, but then she faltered. The expression on Adam Stevens' face had changed. She saw he had lost a little color. For one moment she thought he was looking, why, almost pleadingly at Dr. Richmond and his wife. Then he was shaking their hands enthusiastically, and she decided she must have imagined it.

"Elizabeth, you do not know that Adam is no longer a convict? He has been waiting for a grant of land," Dr. Richmond was saying with a keen look at the other man. "Did your father not tell you?"

"Why, no. How marvelous! I didn't know you were so close to completing your sentence, Adam. Are you not still working for my father then?"

Adam swallowed convulsively, then cleared his throat and said in a choked voice, "Well, in a manner of speaking, I guess I am still working. . ." Then he said more firmly, "Yes, I am still working for your father, Miss Waverley."

"Oh, where is he then? Surely he would not have missed an opportunity to come to Sydney with you?"

Suddenly Mrs. Richmond tapped her on the arm and said quite sharply, "Really, Elizabeth, can't you wait until we get out of this dreadful sun before interrogating this poor man?"

Mrs. Richmond nodded shortly at Adam. "How are you, Adam? Well, I trust. Now, do you think you could get us out of this sad crush? I do declare I am feeling quite faint with the heat. All those months in England made me forget how hot it is here in December so close to Christmas," she added fussily and turned to continue along the wharf.

Elizabeth reluctantly followed her, still staring around, expecting any moment to see her father coming toward them. But she waited until Adam had led them to the shade of a huge warehouse.

Mrs. Richmond was fanning herself vigorously and then looked around haughtily. "My goodness, this place reeks of filth. Why the authorities don't clean this up I'll never know."

Elizabeth was beyond noticing her surroundings. "Now I do not need to bother you anymore, Mrs. Richmond. I will be able to travel home with Father. Oh, I do hope he does not have to stay in Sydney too long. I do so want to go home and see the sweeping plains beyond the ranges where he has taken up more land," she added longingly. "It was one of the reasons I was keen to come home when he told me in his last letter. I have always wondered what the country was like further inland."

She glanced down at her friend, laughing at herself. Mrs. Richmond did not respond. She was staring back at her husband and Adam with a worried frown. Elizabeth followed her gaze and saw that Adam and Dr. Richmond were standing some little distance away. Adam was speaking rapidly in a low murmur. Whatever he was saying made the doctor start. Then they turned and looked at her.

Apprehension gripped Elizabeth. She watched their grave faces as they slowly started toward her, not taking their eyes from her. As she saw the doctor's face more closely, a lump of ice settled deep within her. They stopped in front of her. She looked wildly from the anxious face of the younger man to the shocked, pale face of Dr. Richmond.

"My dear Elizabeth. . ." His voice cracked.

And she knew.

Knew something had happened to her father.

She vaguely realized Mrs. Richmond murmured something in a distressed voice.

Dr. Richmond reached and took her icy hand. "You must be brave, my dear. Your father had an accident. Adam sent a message immediately to you. It would have passed us on our way here."

He took a deep breath, and his hold on her hands tightened.

"I'm so sorry to have to tell you your father died nearly two months ago."

eight

John had once thought nothing could be worse than being locked in the dark, damp, foul hold of the ship for days on end with chains on his feet. But at least there he and Timothy had at times been able to keep up each other's spirits, pray together, even talk about Elizabeth in guarded words.

Now he had chains on his feet in a stinking, small cement cell crowded with far too many convicts, frightened men who could only wonder why they had been separated from the others so abruptly after a few days ashore in their new barracks. And he had not seen Timothy's cheerful, somehow peaceful face since the day Timothy had been marched off alone to some unknown destination.

None of them knew why the irons had been placed on their legs again or why they had been herded together in this small cell. Fear had grown as day after day passed with no information about what was to happen to them. There had been no contact at all with the outside world except for their tight-lipped guards.

John knew it was not what any of them had been told to expect. They had thought they would quickly be put to work on government tasks or even assigned to work for someone. As he'd studied the faces of his cellmates that first day together, he had suddenly realized it must have something to do with the riot aboard the ship. Each man there had been one of those flogged afterward. But if that was the case, he could not understand why Timothy was not with them.

It had been very hard in this place to continue to believe in the loving, caring God Timothy had been teaching him about. But the stories and words of Scripture they had shared for so many weeks were not easy to forget. When his spirits were particularly low, some verses would flash into his mind and somehow bring comfort and encouragement that God was indeed in control of his life, and that above all He would watch over him, would work all things out for good.

But there were still many demons of fear to face and conquer the morning his name was called out and he was roughly marched from the cell. The small room he was at last pushed into was furnished only with a table and chairs. Two men were in the room. One was seated before a pile of papers at one end of the roughly hewn wooden table. He briefly glanced up and returned to wielding his pen.

The other older, gray-haired man swung around from peering out a small, barred window and watched John's shuffling, clanging steps. From his meticulous clothes and haughty demeanor, he was obviously a man of some importance.

John came to a halt in the middle of the room, straightened to his full height, and calmly returned the man's stare. The two guards who had escorted John saluted and withdrew. Then came the sounds of brisk, heavy boots as someone else entered the room behind him.

The well-dressed man did not pause in his careful survey of John's filthy, unkempt appearance and the tattered prison clothes that he had been wearing for far too long without an opportunity to wash either himself or them. Then he muttered something savagely under his breath and strode forward to lean both hands on the table.

"Are those fetters really necessary?" he barked.

"Lieutenant Edwards' orders, sir."

At the short, abrupt words in a familiar voice, John stiffened, swung his head around, and looked straight into the expressionless face of Sergeant Hobbs.

"What's this all about, Sergeant?" he asked sharply. "Why—"

"That's enough, you. You will speak only when spoken to!"

Despite his sharp words, John thought he saw a look of warning in the sergeant's eyes and subsided. Warily he looked again at the other man, who was studying him closely.

"Mr. John Martin?" At John's abrupt nod, his expression tightened, but he said in the same brisk voice, "You would do well to answer me civilly. Have you not been told why you have been brought here, sir?"

"I am a convict," John snarled. "Convicts are not told anything!"

The man raised his head haughtily and stared silently at John. John returned his stare, but something in the man's steady demeanor made him subside and say wearily, "I beg your pardon, sir. I and several other convicts have been kept in a filthy small cell for nearly a week, and we have not been told why or what is to happen to us."

The expression on the man's face changed. A flush of anger rose in his cheeks, and he roared so suddenly that John jumped.

"Lieutenant Edwards again, Sergeant?"

"Yes, sir!"

A fist was brought down heavily on the small table, sending documents flying. The smaller man frantically rescued his pot of ink and scrabbled frantically after the papers. His companion snatched the pen from his clerk's hand, grabbed a piece of paper, and wrote fiercely.

"See that gets to Lieutenant Edwards' superior officer immediately!"

Sergeant Hobbs saluted and swung on his heel. Before he opened the heavy door, he glanced at John and winked. John stared after him in astonishment. What was happening?

"I am Magistrate Hall, and this is my clerk." The man gestured for John to sit on a chair and then sat down himself.

He began to speak very swiftly, and John listened in ever increasing amazement. "On receiving three differing reports, an enquiry is now underway about the conditions and subsequent behavior of all those aboard the *Royal Lady* relating to general treatment of the convicts leading to the riot and its aftermath."

The magistrate shuffled through the now restored pile of documents and then peered at one as he continued. "The reports are from Lieutenant Edwards, Captain Longman, and an extremely interesting one from the well-known and esteemed Dr. Richmond. I see here one of the passengers, ah, yes, a Miss Elizabeth Waverley has also written out her observations. Very clearly, I might add."

John's heart leaped. So she had not forgotten him after all.

Mr. Hall glared at John over the pair of glasses precariously perched on the tip of his nose. "I have been appointed by the board of enquiry to initially interview those involved and obtain their statements."

He paused, and his gaze was suddenly piercing. "Many have already told their stories, Mr. Martin, and you would do well to tell me the truth. Those in the cell with you will also be heard as soon as possible. Now, sir," he said even more abruptly, "tell me your version of events from the time the *Royal Lady* docked at Capetown."

John opened his mouth, but no words came out.

"Come, come, Mr. Martin. Please proceed to tell us your version of events!"

John started, realizing he was still staring in a daze at the man before him. He pushed away thoughts of Elizabeth writing for him, cleared his throat, and started to speak.

He was very cautious when asked for more details about the appalling conditions that developed in the hold of the *Royal Lady* at Capetown and how their hope of relief once the ship had put to sea had gradually faded.

As he spoke, he relived the horror of those days. His voice became harsh, his slight accent more pronounced as he talked and talked. Several times he could not refrain from praising Timothy's attempts to try to calm the panic that began among the convicts as one after the other became very ill.

The clerk scribbled furiously. John only realized much later how cleverly the magistrate had framed his questions whenever John paused briefly, wondering what was wise to say and what to leave out.

When he at last stopped speaking, there was only the

squeak of the clerk's pen. Magistrate Hall sat frowning down at his clasped hands. Then even the pen was still.

John felt suddenly very weary. Would he be believed? Was there a chance he could be hung as he had heard had happened to other convicts who had rebelled with violence?

The magistrate raised his head and searched John's face intently. "Can you name the leaders who actually started the attack on the guards and tried to seize their weapons?"

John stiffened. "I couldn't really name anyone specifically. I cannot even say that the man who was shot was a ringleader, even though he happened to be just in front of me when he was hit. Almost every man jack of them was ready to try anything. They were convinced they were going to die anyway and had worked themselves up to believe they may as well die trying to get out to the fresh air."

"But surely they knew they were out to sea, a long way from land, and they had no chance of taking over the ship!"

John closed his eyes for a moment. Once again he was back in the horror of the sweltering heat of the fetid, dark hold, his throat parched, his stomach churning at the revolting smells, trying desperately himself to hang onto his sanity.

He raised his head slowly and stared blindly in front of him. "Sir, you would have to realize how dark, how dreadful our situation was. The first few weeks after we left England had been hard enough, but nothing like what we were experiencing then. The heat was stifling, men were falling sick everywhere. Then that man died, and despite the surgeon's efforts others seemed close to death. They felt all hope was gone."

"And what about you and this Mr. Timothy Hardy you keep referring to?" There was a sneer in Mr. Hall's voice. "Are you trying to tell me either of you were any different? You use the word *they*. Why should I believe you two were any different?"

John looked straight at the magistrate. He was watching John very closely, and strangely there was no hint of derision in his eyes.

"Because Timothy, a small, frail man, had such a strong

personal faith in God, and somehow he helped me to have some too," John said simply.

Something flashed in the magistrate's eyes before he looked down at the table. For a moment John thought the long, tense hours since he had arrived in this strange land must be causing him to see things that could not possibly be there, like a gleam of respect in this magistrate for a convicted murderer.

John continued in an expressionless voice, explaining in more detail how Lieutenant Edwards had ordered his soldiers to put down the riot and had himself shot the convict. The soldiers had used their rifle butts ruthlessly, and it was still a marvel to John that they had not all opened fire. Perhaps they had seen how weak and helpless the desperate, emaciated men had been.

After John reached the end of his account, Mr. Hall sat strangely still. Then in a very low voice he observed, "You have not yet told me of your punishment."

John went still. He opened his mouth, but no words would come out. The memory of the pain and humiliation of the flogging would never leave him if he lived to be a hundred.

"At least tell me how many lashes you received, Mr. Martin." The voice was still low but nonetheless demanded a response.

John's mouth was strangely dry. He swallowed and at last said harshly, "It is not something I like to think about, sir. I believe there were over sixty."

The man stared at him with a frown. "You only believe?"

John forced himself to smile slightly. "Others told me so. After a while I did not hear the count."

There was silence for a long moment as Mr. Hall bent his head over his pen and paper. "Would you consider it too much of an intrusion to show me your back, Mr. Martin?"

John stared at him. After so many months of being ordered about as though he were mere dirt, to hear the man's soft, apologetic request sounded strange. Then Mr. Hall raised his eyes, and John saw compassion and sympathy. Suddenly his heart swelled with hope. It was the first time he had met anyone in authority besides Dr. Richmond who seemed to understand.

John rose slowly, turned around, and eased off his shirt. He had not seen his back, but the swiftly sucked in breath of both men told him that the newly healed scars he could only touch must look even worse than he thought.

Not once during his interview had he mentioned Elizabeth. Now memories of a woman's tender hands ministering to those wounds scorched through him. He had been trying hard for many long weeks not to think of Elizabeth so he would not go mad with longing.

Always he had to battle the bitterness that tried to take over him when he thought of what might have been if he were not a convict. He saw no hope of ever proving his innocence now so far away from Yorkshire, and he looked on her sincere words as the wishful thinking of the sweet, inexperienced young woman she was.

The interview was abruptly terminated. Magistrate Hall rose and said shortly, "Thank you, Mr. Martin. You have been very helpful. I may need to speak to you again, but that will be all for now."

John found himself marched back to the cell by the same silent guards. He was not entirely surprised to find the other convicts in a ferment of excitement. Shortly after he had been taken away, all their leg irons had been removed and they had been allowed plenty of water to wash in and been issued new clothes. One of them had had the presence of mind to ask for a set for the man they now crowded around, clamoring to hear what had happened. But most of them greeted what he told them with expressions of dismay and sullen anger.

Later that night as he tossed restlessly, John for the first time let his iron will relax and thought about Elizabeth. Her sweet face and tender smile haunted him. He smiled as he pictured her glorious red-gold hair that fell in ringlets when not tied back as she had leaned across him. He thought he smelled again her sweet perfume.

As he tried to shut out his grim surroundings by closing his eyes, he saw again those incredibly green eyes flashing with so many emotions. They had darkened when she had been bewildered or upset and blazed green fire when furiously angry, as they had when he had mentioned Beth.

Several times he had thought of Beth since his new relationship with God. Timothy had helped him to come to the point where he could ask genuinely for forgiveness for all his bitterness toward her. When he at last had been able to forgive Beth, even to pray for her, a tremendous burden had fallen from him.

And many times during these last few weeks, he had prayed earnestly for Elizabeth. Now he prayed again for her until sleep freed him from his tumultuous thoughts. Then it was her eyes, softened, damp with tears, and filled with love for him that he dreamed of.

Events moved swiftly after that initial interview. A few days later the court hearing commenced before an impressive bench of magistrates, including Mr. Hall. To John's dismay and increasing concern, Timothy was not present. Except for the two women, all the other major participants were there.

Lieutenant Edwards crisply and haughtily gave his version of events, but his haughtiness swiftly changed to anger as first Sergeant Hobbs and then Captain Longman verified the convicts' statements, telling of his neglect of the convicts under his care. John watched the lieutenant's face twist into a sneer as Elizabeth's statement was read. The look of hatred he turned on John made him go suddenly cold. This man's nature was even more vicious than he had thought possible.

Then Lieutenant Edwards' anger turned to fear as he was completely humiliated by Dr. Richmond's version of events. Most of the magistrates on the bench treated Dr. Richmond as an old friend, and it was obvious to all that both the captain and the lieutenant had sadly underestimated Dr. Richmond's standing in the colony.

Within a couple weeks, John was visited by a jubilant

Sergeant Hobbs, who had come to say farewell before taking an extended leave at his small farm at Parramatta.

"Lieutenant Edwards has been demoted to sergeant and transferred to Van Dieman's Land, so I hope we've seen the last of him," he told John. "I doubt too if that Captain Longman will be given another convict transport contract."

"Have you heard what will happen to the rest of us? Do you know where Timothy Hardy is?" John asked urgently. Rumors had been flying thick and fast among the convicts, one of them that those who had started the riot might yet be hung.

The sergeant's lined faced became grave. "I believe Mr. Hardy has been assigned to a farmer," he said abruptly. "But some of them ringleaders have cause to be afraid. I've heard they may be shipped to the penal settlement of Norfolk Island where last year conditions were so bad there was a dreadful mutiny and attempt to escape. Many were killed, and later thirteen convicts were hanged."

He paused, and then his face lightened. "Don't worry about you being one of them," he said hurriedly. "I think they believed my word about you saving my very own skin."

As foolish as he knew he was, John had kept hoping against hope that Elizabeth might find some way to visit him. Desperately he longed to ask the sergeant if he had heard anything of her, but he managed to keep silent.

It was another few days before he found out the sergeant's predictions had been correct. Several frightened and sullen convicts—those who had inflicted the worst injuries to some of the soldiers—were marched off to board a ship for dreaded Norfolk Island. Another day passed before John was curtly told he had been assigned and ordered to collect his belongings.

As he carefully rolled up his meager belongings, his mind was filled with turmoil. He lifted up his heavy heart in silent prayer. Despite his frequent requests for information, he had not been told one word of what was happening to Timothy, and he wondered if he would ever see him again.

"You've been assigned to a good master, so make sure

you work hard and keep yourself out of trouble," he was warned roughly before at last being thrust outside into the bright sunlight.

A tall, handsome man about his own age and dressed in smart town clothes was waiting impatiently. Nearby was a well-laden dray drawn by two large, restless horses.

"There you are at last," the man said sharply. "Get aboard. We're late."

John threw his small pack behind the small, hunched-over driver who was very busy trying to keep his two charges quiet. The driver's face was hidden beneath a large straw hat.

"Good morning, John. Glad you could join us."

At the quiet voice filled with a mixture of excitement and amusement, he froze. Then he turned slowly and stared at the neatly dressed driver. Bright eyes and a beaming face were observing him closely.

"Timothy? Why, Timothy. . ." Words failed him, but both his hands shot out to eagerly grasp the slim one being extended toward him.

"Well, are you going to stay here all day?" the stranger snapped. "For myself, the faster we leave this place behind us and smell the free, clean air of the bush, the better. Get those horses moving!"

John watched in a daze as Timothy loosened his grip on the reins and the horses started forward.

They were soon moving at a brisk pace, and as Timothy skillfully tooled the reins to dodge the traffic in the busy streets, he murmured, "Don't worry about Mr. Stevens' short tongue. He wanted to be well on the road by now. He has been all that is good and kind. A strange, silent man, he seems to really hate being near the jail. I believe he only finished serving his own sentence last year, and I guess prisons still make him a trite edgy."

"Do you know where we are headed?" John asked at last after the sheer wonder, surprise, and overwhelming relief at being with Timothy again had died away enough for him to have control of his voice.

Then suddenly he wondered, and by no means for the first time, just what it was about this small, insignificant-looking man that had drawn him to so want to be with him. Certainly Timothy had been almost overwhelming in his gratitude for saving his son, but that alone had not been the reason they had become friends.

And then as he watched the beaming smile flood Timothy's face, John realized it was because in the misery and suffering they had shared, this man had loved him. Even when he had cursed and sworn at the injustices done to him, even in his darkest hours, this little man had loved him.

As Jesus had? As Jesus did even now?

John sat a little straighter. The fact that God loved him seemed more real.

Timothy had not answered his question immediately. He was guiding the horses carefully to avoid a dust-covered stagecoach, and when John glanced again at his friend's face, his heart sank to see a frown creasing his forehead.

"No, I don't know where we're going, not really," Timothy said slowly, "except that Dr. Richmond assured me that this Adam Stevens is a good man and has a new property on the western plains the other side of a place called Bathurst. Has some cattle, but mainly sheep, he said."

"You've spoken with Dr. Richmond?"

Timothy looked at him with some surprise. "Yes, of course. Why, didn't he come to see you?"

"No," John said shortly. "The only time I've seen him was in that court of enquiry one day. I was surprised you were not there, in fact. Haven't heard one word about what was happening to any of us."

Timothy's frown deepened. "Oh, I was there all right, but obviously not at the same time as yourself. But that's strange, Dr. Richmond not seeing you. He did sound very concerned for you when he came and saw me both before and after that court of enquiry."

Elizabeth.

Pain swept through John. The wise old doctor in his own way was trying to protect Elizabeth from her concern for a convicted murderer with a life sentence.

After a short silence, John said abruptly, "Fill me in on what you know about the results of that enquiry."

"You mean you don't know?"

There was such amazement in Timothy's voice that John looked at him sharply. "Only that our friend Lieutenant Edwards has been demoted and transferred to Van Dieman's Land. Some of the men were sent to Norfolk Island."

A shadow crossed Timothy's face. Then a huge smile transformed him. But it faded abruptly, and he looked away.

Alarm flashed through John. "Timothy? What's wrong?"

"Nothing's wrong, but I don't know how to tell you that I. . . I've been given a ticket-of-leave."

A momentary pang of envy shot through John. All convicts knew what a ticket-of-leave meant. Timothy no longer had to work as an assigned man for a master and was free from the government claims of forced labor. He had to stay in the colony but could work for himself wherever he wanted to, earn money, start a new life, even if the knowledge hung over him that he had to live an exemplary life so it would be renewed every twelve months.

"Why, Timothy, that's absolutely marvelous." John shot out his hand and wrung Timothy's hand once more. "But I thought that if there was any chance of getting one it would not be until after several years of a sentence had been served."

Two spots of color rose in Timothy's usually pale face. "Dr. Richmond convinced them. Apparently he told them that he did not know what he would have done without the help of both of us throughout the whole voyage, and that instead of being thanked we had been so cruelly punished."

Timothy paused, and then he added in a rush, "I didn't know how to tell you. It doesn't seem fair that I was given one and not you when you were the one who tried so hard to prevent the soldiers from being hurt and were then punished so. . .so severely. Dr. Richmond told me there was considerable debate about you, but they decided that I had only been sent here on a short term for political infringements. You. . . you were a. . .a murderer."

John was silent while he tried to deal with the old pain once more. Even if somehow he were to prove his innocence, would that label follow him until he died?

"And with my size and strength I'm a danger to society," he said roughly at last and gave a bitter laugh.

"But this Adam fellow seemed quite happy to have you assigned to him," Timothy said quickly.

"Probably because he is taking us to the wilderness out west and he thinks there's little mischief to get up to there."

After a long pause, John asked softly, "Was Elizabeth ever mentioned?"

Timothy shook his head sadly. "Once I ventured to ask Dr. Richmond about her. He became very haughty, even angry. Said it was best if we forgot all about her."

John stared blindly ahead. *Forget her? If only that were possible!*

They were silent after that. John wondered wearily just what was ahead of them. There had been a lot of rumors and speculation about the country west of the ranges and the danger from savage aboriginals. There were still vast tracts of land in the west that no white man had ever set foot on.

As they left Sydney and then Parramatta, John's heart was heavy. He was relieved and thankful to be with Timothy, to be out in the fresh air, to be assigned to a master who was proving to be courteous and kindly.

He offered up even more thanks to a provident God when they passed a convict road gang working and repairing the dangerous, narrow road winding its way over the Blue Mountains. They were guarded by bored soldiers with fixed bayonets. With a shudder, John could only imagine the conditions they lived and worked under.

But every plodding step of the horses was taking him farther from the one person he longed so desperately to be with. He was feeling sad and hurt that, despite her earnest protestations of wanting to prove his innocence and even her written testimony in court, not once had Elizabeth sent him a message. It was no surprise she had not been allowed to visit him, but surely she could have found some way of contacting him.

By the time they had set up camp that first night, Adam Stevens had relaxed. "Ah, it is so good to be out of the city again," he said simply after he had shown them how he wanted things set up and how to build and light a safe camp-fire in the hot summer.

As he later told them about the bush and their destination out west, his new sheep station, he completely lost his reserve. He also warned them of some of the dangers of the bush.

"Always keep an eye out for snakes," he said finally, and then gave a bark of laughter as both Timothy and John intently surveyed their immediate surroundings.

They looked at each other a little sheepishly but then laughed with him. And it was so good to laugh again, especially out here with only the dark bush and the startled birds and wildlife to hear.

John was amazed at how quickly the light disappeared completely in comparison to the long evenings in Yorkshire. He said so, and Adam stopped poking at the small fire he had placed a blackened tin container on to make tea and looked at him steadily.

"It's not like home here," he said quietly. "No long summer days, but then no long winter nights either. When Mr.—" He stopped abruptly.

After a long pause, as he stared at the leaping flames, he said slowly, "Especially when I first went right out west, the land seemed so vast, so flat in comparison to England. The trees and bushes are not the same bright greens. Not many at all have leaves that change color and fall. But I hope you will find like I have that there is a beauty, a tranquillity, a healing in this vast land so different from England."

There was nostalgia in his voice, and all three were silent until the billy boiled and they were eating some of the bread and mutton from the food supplies. After a while Adam continued telling them what they should expect in the months ahead.

Then John asked something that he had been wondering about off and on all day. "Mr. Stevens, from what you have said, it will be a hard life out on this new property of yours. Timothy said you finished serving your time a year or so ago. Have you no wish to return home to your family?"

Adam Stevens gave a harsh laugh. "Home? I no longer have a home or family who cares in England. There's nothing there for me anymore." He stood up and threw the last of his tea into the dying embers of the fire. "You'd better get some sleep," he snapped. "We break camp as soon as it's light. Oh, and don't call me 'Mister.' Adam will do."

The days and nights rolled by until at last they arrived and set up camp near the Gordon homestead on the Bathurst plains. Adam told them he had been able to purchase several hundred head of sheep from the friendly owner of the station, and that he had already purchased many more at another property in the area.

"They are being held for me there, and I'm leaving you here to mind this flock while I go and fetch them."

John had been looking at the bleating sheep and protested quickly, "We had sheep where I grew up in Spain, but I don't know anything about the care of sheep here."

Adam looked at him thoughtfully and then smiled grimly. "That's another reason to leave you here. I've made arrangements for my old friend, Will Gordon, to give you some lessons. Once we're out west, you'll be learning the hard way if I'm not around."

So, learn they did. And there was much to learn about the right pastures, crutching, detailing lambs, protection from blowflies, how to use the blades that cut the greasy valuable fleece from the backs of belligerent sheep. They listened meekly, asking a few questions but realizing it could take them a lifetime to learn all there was to know.

Both men thought Adam had been strangely reticent about his movements, but by the time he returned several days later with more men and more sheep, both Timothy and John were too glad to be on the move again to ask too many questions. More supplies had also been obtained from wherever Adam had been, a place they were rather puzzled that the usually friendly man refused bluntly to talk about.

The supplies had been loaded on a long wagon pulled by a team of bullocks. The old, wizened bullock driver stared them up and down, spat out a clump of tobacco on the ground, mumbled a couple of words that included a swearword and "new chums" before ambling off to attend his charges.

"At least he didn't call us convicts," John said with amusement as he and Timothy looked at each other.

As they let the sheep graze on the journey west, day after day slipped slowly by. And gradually the long, quiet days did start to bring their own healing.

But try as he might, John could never completely banish the image of red-gold hair framing the beautiful face of Elizabeth. Her soft voice and flashing green eyes continued to haunt his dreams.

Had her reunion with her father been as sweet as she had hoped? Was she enjoying the wide open spaces she had told them about? He often wished she had told him just where her home was. All he knew was that it was at least two or three hours on horseback from Parramatta.

Timothy often talked nostalgically about his wife and small son. Somehow John could not bring himself to speak out loud about Elizabeth. In his dreams she was his alone to admire, to dare to love. And sometimes when he awoke and knew he might never see her again, that reality was almost more than he could cope with.

nine

January 1837

"My dear Elizabeth, what a delightful surprise! How truly lovely to see you again after all this time. But how could you travel all this way without your companion? I trust that my dear cousin is well?"

Elizabeth nodded and returned Mrs. Richmond's embrace with enthusiasm. She forced a smile as that good woman held her by the shoulders, studied her carefully, and without waiting for an answer said, "There is still a shadow in those beautiful green eyes, my dear, but I'm glad that you have put away those dull mourning gowns of yours at last." Although she spoke in her usual forthright way, she smiled gently.

Elizabeth squeezed her hand once more before letting her lead the way into the cool shadows of the house. "Well, it is twelve months since. . .since we arrived home on the *Royal Lady*," she said quietly.

Mrs. Richmond paused momentarily and then said quickly, "Would you like a cold drink or a cup of tea to refresh you?" She sank onto a chair and fanned herself vigorously.

"Oh, definitely a cold drink to start with. I declare this must be the hottest January we've had."

Elizabeth watched with some interest as Mrs. Richmond gave brisk, detailed instructions to the neatly uniformed servant who had been quietly waiting in the background.

When the servant had scurried away, Elizabeth said, "Yes, it has been hot. The river is getting dangerously low for the stock, although they do say there has been rain in the hills and it may improve. But enough of that," she added hastily. "All we seem to talk about lately is the weather. I am afraid your cousin is recovering from a slight fever, and I left in such haste she was unable to accompany me."

She smiled slightly at Mrs. Richmond's frown and added, "I was quite safe with one of my women, and a couple of my men escorted us. How is Dr. Richmond?"

"I'm sure he will be very happy to see you, but he does take his guardianship of you very seriously. I'm sure I don't know what he will say about your coming without Sarah."

"He must realize that in another few weeks I will be of age and can then do as I please."

Mrs. Richmond looked taken aback at the sharpness of her words.

Elizabeth forced a smile, and after swallowing rapidly, Mrs. Richmond said swiftly, "Dr. Richmond is quite well, although he too is worried about the lack of rain and keeps talking about visiting our property at Bathurst even though the manager is so excellent. But he has been very busy here on this small farm, and then of course there has been all this debate about self-government for New South Wales as well as the abolition of transportation." She stopped abruptly and bit her lip.

Elizabeth had stiffened but managed to keep the smile on her face as she said calmly, "I think that far too many land-holders fear the shortage of labor in the bush if they can no longer get assigned convicts. One doubts if very many newly arrived immigrants would be very willing to travel so far from Sydney and all their comforts."

She stopped speaking as the servant entered with a tray of refreshments and watched as Mrs. Richmond said, "Thank you, Mrs. Hughes. I trust you have settled well into your new quarters?"

The woman bobbed a curtsey. "Yes, thank ye, ma'am. It be very beautiful."

She beamed at her mistress so worshipfully before bustling off about her duties that Elizabeth gave a low laugh. "Another woman from the Female Factory at Parramatta?"

Her friend handed her a glass of fresh orange juice and then looked at her serenely. "Of course, and as always, I had her thoroughly investigated. And how many convicts do you have working for you now, may I ask?"

Elizabeth smiled impishly at her. "As many reputable ones as I can find work for, of course." Her smile faded. "However, there are none that I can trust as we could Adam Stevens."

Mrs. Richmond had just lifted her glass to her lips, but suddenly she choked. "Oh, dear, how clumsy of me," she said fussily as she dabbed at the juice that had spilled down her gown. "My new maid will be very cross at having to clean this again so soon. I do declare she only just finished repairing and cleaning it yesterday." A blush had stained Mrs. Richmond's cheeks.

It was not like Elizabeth's friend to be so upset by such a small incident. Elizabeth's heart leaped. So she did know.

She carefully put down her own glass. "Have you recently heard anything of Adam, Mrs. Richmond?" she asked brightly. "I was so disappointed last year when he had already left for the outback before our business in Sydney was completed." She paused and added, "Oh, by the way, I saw our mutual neighbor, Mrs. Gordon, a couple days ago."

Mrs. Richmond was still avoiding looking at her, but at that name she started.

Elizabeth smiled and added sweetly, "You do remember Mrs. Gordon, don't you? Their huge property runs down to our southern boundary. She has such a tribe of children she very rarely leaves home. She asked after Adam and the two men he left with them while he came to Waverley Station for our sheep to take to my father's new property, or rather, Adam's new property now. Remember," she added sweetly, "the one Father left Adam in his will?"

With considerable interest, Elizabeth saw her friend give such a start her cup of tea tilted alarmingly. Elizabeth continued in her bright, conversational tones, saying, "Mrs. Gordon was all effusive cordiality. She assured me that at least we could feel comfortable that the two convicts he had with him seemed decent enough, had quite captured all with their pleasant ways, despite their appalling ignorance of how to cope in the bush. They were so newly arrived from England, you see."

To Elizabeth's immense satisfaction, Mrs. Richmond suddenly put down her cup with a rattle. In a suddenly sharp voice Elizabeth added, "How is it that no one told me about those two men Adam brought back from Sydney?"

Mrs. Richmond began tearing at a handkerchief in her lap.

"She couldn't remember their names," Elizabeth continued, "only having met them briefly before being brought to bed with her tenth child. Apparently one convict, a small, insignificant-looking man had a ticket-of-leave, but the other one. . ."

Elizabeth took a deep breath and stared challengingly at Mrs. Richmond, who was now watching her with a resigned expression.

"The other one was so handsome, so Spanish-looking with his black curly hair and unusual blue eyes, that all the ladies in the place were in a twitter."

Mrs. Richmond stared at her and then gave a deep sigh. "I told Dr. Richmond you would find out," she muttered.

"It was John Martin and Timothy Hardy, wasn't it?" Elizabeth's voice had risen.

Mrs. Richmond studied her carefully and nodded.

Elizabeth suddenly sprang to her feet. "Do you have any idea how often the last twelve months I've tried to find out what happened to them? Beyond telling me about Timothy's ticket-of-leave and that John had been assigned you. . .you knew nothing you said. Nothing! You knew, and neither of you said a word. Not a word!" She wrung her hands together. "I suppose my notes to John were never delivered either?"

Mrs. Richmond shook her head reluctantly.

"Oh, what must he be thinking of me? Not even a message since we left the ship!" Elizabeth burst out. "All his life people have failed him, and now I have too!"

"Elizabeth, sit down!"

Her friend's voice was so forceful, Elizabeth stopped her pacing and stared.

"That attitude of yours is the very reason why Dr. Richmond forbade me to tell you he had arranged for John Martin to be assigned to Adam Stevens. It seemed providential that he was leaving immediately for the outback, too good an opportunity to miss."

Mrs. Richmond sighed. "Elizabeth," she continued in much gentler tones, "you must know that any fondness you may have for a man serving a life sentence has absolutely no hope of. . .of. . ."

She stopped, and Elizabeth felt the heat staining her cheeks. Very slowly she sank down into her chair, her head bowed. Suddenly a sob shook her, and then the tears started to trickle down her face.

Mrs. Richmond was on her feet in a flash. "My dear girl, I do feel for you, but this will not do, it really will not do."

When Elizabeth's pent-up tears had ceased and she had been petted and embraced by a very upset Mrs. Richmond, she at last lifted her chin and said firmly, "John Martin is a very fine man, and I have many times asked God to help me forget him, but instead, my longing to see him again continues to grow. I am not a fool, I know how impossible it all is, and yet. . ."

She paused, not sure how her friend would respond to her other news. "I immediately wanted to start making preparations to travel out to visit. . .visit Adam, but our neighbor had also brought some mail to me that had been delivered to them by mistake. One was from Timothy's wife. I have written to her a couple of times. This letter told me she had heard from Timothy at last. He had written just before leaving Sydney to work for a very kind man called Adam Stevens, but she was not sure if his address in the country meant it would be possible for her letter to reach him by the time she and her son arrived in Sydney.

"Her letter had even taken a long time to reach me, and I thought I should confront Dr. Richmond first and see if you had any more information. Also, it seems the *Royal Admiral* was to leave only a few days after she had posted this letter. I am worried about her and decided before I went to find John that I should talk to you first about him, and also to ask if you could look out for her."

Mrs. Richmond stared at her. To Elizabeth's relief she did not immediately comment on her proposed trip to the outback, but exclaimed, "Timothy Hardy's wife!" Then her eyes narrowed. "And how could she find the money for. . ." She paused and eyed Elizabeth thoughtfully. "You sent it to her, didn't you?" she asked bluntly.

Elizabeth hesitated and then said shortly. "It was nothing. You know that my father has left me quite a wealthy woman."

"That was very well done of you, Elizabeth." Mrs. Richmond's voice was full of admiration. "So, she should be arriving soon. How wonderful for Mr. Hardy." She stopped short and said slowly, "Now, just a moment, what did you say was the name of the ship?"

"The *Royal Admiral*."

"Why, I do believe that is the name of the ship that Dr. Richmond mentioned only this morning. He is expecting news from London about the push for self-government and was quite excited that the ship had been seen anchored off the heads last night, waiting to enter the harbor at first light."

Elizabeth's eyes widened. "Oh, that poor woman, imagine how bewildered she must be in all the hustle and bustle at the wharf." She jumped up. "I must go and meet her."

Mrs. Richmond insisted on accompanying her, but when they arrived, the passengers were already disembarking.

"Oh, I do hope we have not missed her," Elizabeth exclaimed as she craned her head to try and see through the crowd.

The back of a tall man with short, curly black hair caught her attention for a moment. He looked so much like John Martin that she stared at his neat, country clothes for a moment, and then looked blindly away. So many times before she had thought she had seen him, even once in a long line of convicts being marched past her coach.

She continued searching the crowd, but her eyes were drawn back to the tall man. He turned his head, and suddenly looked toward her. For one moment she thought that mentioning John Martin to someone for the first time in months was causing her to conjure him up. His gaze swept over her and then suddenly he started. His eyes widened in unbelief.

Their eyes clung.

She stood motionless, hardly daring to breathe. Then she saw him straighten his shoulders. He started pushing through the crowd toward her.

"Why, I do declare, isn't that Mr. Hardy over there?" Mrs. Richmond panted beside her.

Elizabeth hardly heard her. That other familiar face loomed ever closer. Then he was in front of her. She was vaguely aware that Mrs. Richmond gave a startled gasp of recognition, but not once did she stop staring into John's blue eyes until he executed a very gentlemanly bow. But he said not a word, just stood there waiting for her to either turn away or acknowledge him.

She could not move, just stare at him wildly. His face had filled out, his skin was even darker from being in the hot sun. He looked fit and well. He looked absolutely wonderful.

His eyes suddenly changed from startled pleasure and wonder to pools of pain. He moved a step back, and she was startled into extending her hand to him.

"John, why John, it is you. For a moment I thought. . .I thought I must be dreaming." Her voice sounded as breathless and excited as she felt.

His face lit up. Her hand was enveloped by his strong, darkly tanned one. He lifted it to his lips. It was far from being a conventional gesture. His lips caressed her fingertips, and she began to tremble. His grip on her hand tightened convulsively.

"Elizabeth, Miss Waverley. . ." He paused, and she saw him swallow, realizing suddenly that he was as affected as she was.

"Oh, Miss Waverley, Miss Waverley," another emotion-filled voice intruded. "My wife. . .my wife's here, and Tim. They are actually here!"

John dropped her hand as though he had been stung and took a step back.

Elizabeth was still bereft of words. She stared at him until a tearful, excited voice behind her said, "Miss Waverley? Oh Miss, how can I ever thank you?"

Elizabeth swung around and was suddenly enveloped by warm young arms.

"I was in the very depths of despair when your first letter arrived. There had been no word from my Timothy. Not a word, although his letters to me did arrive at last in one big heap," Mrs. Hardy babbled on. "And then when the money arrived. . .I. . .I. . ."

Her voice faded away as big tears started streaming down her cheeks. With a helpless gesture, she turned to her husband again, who immediately put his arm around her, saying in a voice as tearful as hers, "Now, now Molly, my dear, now, now. Don't start the waterworks again. You'll upset young Tim."

Elizabeth, still unable to speak, stared at them for a moment and then her gaze went back to John's strong, handsome features. He was staring at her, but looked down as a small voice said loudly, "Why, aren't you the man who pulled me out of the water?"

As he bent to greet young Tim, his face lit up in such a breathtakingly beautiful smile that Elizabeth swallowed sharply and looked away. Her gaze encountered her friend's worried face, and she took a grip on herself.

"It's really lovely to see you arrived safely, Mrs. Hardy," she said huskily, "but do let me introduce you to my friend, Mrs. Richmond."

Mrs. Richmond raised an eyebrow. To Elizabeth's relief she said politely, "How do you do, Mrs. Hardy?"

Timothy's wife pulled away from his sheltering arm and finished using his large handkerchief to mop up her face. She beamed at Mrs. Richmond and bobbed a curtsey. "Oh, you are the wife of the doctor who was so kind to my husband. How can I ever. . .ever thank you all. . .I. . .I. . ."

Seeing the danger of more tears, Elizabeth said quickly, "And I'm sure there will be opportunities later to say all that has to be said."

She faltered for a brief moment as her gaze encountered John's unsmiling one. Then she straightened and asked in a firmer voice, "Where are you staying? I'm sure Adam would not mind if we joined you so we could enjoy a good talk." She looked around. "He is with you, isn't he?"

"Adam left on a ship for England not so very long ago." John's voice was harsh, his expression guarded. "We have been staying at an inn well on the way to Parramatta."

Elizabeth stared at him in astonishment. "England! But I thought he had vowed never to return there."

"His uncle has died. To Adam's utter astonishment he is joint heir with his brother of a considerable estate. His brother demanded his return to sort out their affairs. Adam has left us in charge of Stevens Downs until he returns," he added with a proud lift of his head.

"But I thought—" Elizabeth stopped short, realizing she was about to reveal information she had been told in confidence one lonely winter's night by the young convict suffering so badly from homesickness and despair.

It seemed that Adam was after all going to see the brother he had thought never to see again. But that was his business. This was a new country, a new life. What did old history really matter to anyone else except the one concerned?

"This is neither the time nor place for a conversation about Adam's doings," Mrs. Richmond said briskly. "Now, what about all returning to my home for refreshments. It is also on the road to Parramatta. We all do have quite a bit to talk about."

Elizabeth looked at her with gratitude. It was so typical of her kindhearted friend. She gave most people the impression of being very proper and correct, but here she was, inviting two convicts to her home as though they were honored guests. She risked another glance at John and saw the utter astonishment in his face. He at least realized the full import of the invitation.

It was obvious that Timothy Hardy did also. "Why, Mrs. Richmond, ma'am, I. . .we. . .we could not impose on you," he stammered. He paused and then said with considerable dignity, "We do thank you for your condescension, but we yet have to see to the unloading of our belongings, and we will need to get settled at the inn before night falls."

Mrs. Richmond hesitated for only a moment before taking a deep breath and turning to the other man. "And what about you, Mr. Martin? Are you free to accept my invitation? I do believe Elizabeth wants to speak to you about something."

John's eyes widened in amazement, and then he glanced swiftly at Elizabeth. Once again her friend had taken her breath away. She felt the color rise in her cheeks.

"I promised Timothy to help him with their belongings, ma'am," he said hesitantly.

"Of course," Mrs. Richmond said briskly, "but I'm sure that once they're settled they would prefer to spend some time alone. Perhaps you could visit with us this evening."

Still John hesitated, and Elizabeth said swiftly, "I believe you said that Dr. Richmond would not be home until late tonight, Mrs. Richmond?"

A flash of gratitude for her understanding flashed into his face. Mrs. Richmond paused only momentarily before assuring him that was so.

"I'm sure we all have much to talk about," she added politely. "I'd very much like to hear firsthand how Adam's new station is going."

Elizabeth took much care with her appearance for the evening. She had fortunately packed one of her best dresses for the trip, knowing that the Richmonds lived such an active social life she might well need it even for a brief visit.

All her unusual primping and fussing before her mirror was amply rewarded by the gleam of admiration and then delight that filled John's face as his gaze swept over the rich, green dress that emphasized the green of her eyes, and her artfully arranged red-gold curls.

She felt heat sweep through her in a tide and knew by the smile that suddenly sparkled from his dark eyes that the color had risen into her cheeks.

Being the gracious hostess she was, Mrs. Richmond greeted John pleasantly. Not for a moment did she betray that all the way home from Sydney she had desperately tried to talk Elizabeth out of becoming involved again in his affairs and only yielded defeat when Elizabeth had said strongly, "There is naught you can say or do to change my mind. People have let John Martin down all his life. Before God, I refuse to be another."

After he had taken the seat indicated by their hostess, he said politely, "I trust your father is pleased to have you home, Miss Waverley?"

She had thought some months ago that she had shed so many tears for her father that she could have no tears left for him. Now she felt their sudden sting again at the unexpected question.

She bent her head and with gratitude heard Mrs. Richmond say softly, "Unfortunately our dear friend was killed a couple months before we arrived from England. We only found out the day the ship arrived."

John gave an exclamation of distress.

Mrs. Richmond rose suddenly, said briskly, "I need to see our cook about tomorrow's menus, and you young people have much to speak of," and whisked herself from the room.

There was a tense silence for a long moment. Elizabeth sat staring down at her hands, still fighting the tears at the memory of her double grief at losing the two men she cared so much about. Then suddenly John moved and crossed the room to sit beside her on the brocade-covered couch.

"I'm so very sorry about your father, Elizabeth."

She slowly raised her head. "I so wanted him to meet you, John."

Surprise shone at her from his dark eyes. Then he scowled. "I hardly think your father would have been interested in meeting a convict."

"You're very wrong, John." She paused and then said steadily, "Do you remember that I once told you I was already friendly with four convicts?" After he had given a brief, reluctant nod, she said simply, "My father was very young when he was transported to Australia."

Shock held him rigid. At last he said slowly, "I would imagine that would be all the more reason he would not have wanted his own daughter to befriend convicts."

She hesitated before saying reluctantly, "I'm afraid you are probably right, but now we'll never know." After a pause she said thoughtfully, "But my father was a very shrewd judge of character. I think he would have wanted to help you if he had let himself get to know you."

"How can you possibly know what kind of a man I am?"

"I know."

John continued to stare at her. He shook his head in disbelief. How could this woman stand there looking at him from such steady, confident eyes? Never before had anyone except perhaps Timothy and more recently Adam Stevens demonstrated such faith in him.

"No dishonorable man risks his life to save a stranger's small child from drowning or earns the respect and admiration of a tough soldier like Sergeant Hobbs and hundreds of fellow convicts." She paused and then added softly, "And only a very good man will suffer as you did for his friend."

He was speechless, unable to tear his eyes from her as she rose and came closer.

"But I am so very sorry I couldn't find you all those months." Briefly she explained, and the sadness and regret that swept into her face as she spoke confounded him even more.

"You tried to find me?"

She nodded briefly. Tears moistened her eyes, and he held his breath willing her silently not to cry. He couldn't bear to see her cry. Her tears threatened to melt the hard core that had been deep inside him for so long despite his new relationship with God.

He was thankful when she brushed a hand almost angrily across her eyes and turned abruptly away.

"Everyone I approached confessed complete ignorance about the fate of the two convicts exonerated of bad behavior after the enquiry. All I could discover was that they had been assigned and moved out to work in the bush. That was what Dr. Richmond told me himself," she finished angrily. "My father made him my guardian. Now I know it was at his instigation that the information was kept from me. He even failed to deliver my letters to you."

She had written to him!

"But Adam told us it was he who organized the whole thing." John stopped abruptly, wishing he had held his tongue as she swung back and he saw her flashing eyes.

"I know. I only found out a few days ago where you were."

She told him how she had found out, and when she at last fell silent, he said quietly, "I can well understand their desire to protect you. You would have been especially vulnerable at that time."

"Mrs. Richmond told me all about it this morning," she said sadly. "Apparently Adam was sworn to secrecy and has been faithfully reporting how you are to them."

"Adam has become a good friend." John hesitated for a moment, wondering if it was wise to get her hopes up, but he was still rather dazed and too full of wonder at God's workings in his life himself to keep it all bottled in any longer.

So he blurted out, "While he is in England he has promised to see if he can recover the Bible and the letters of my mother I tried to have delivered to my father during my trial. Adam will speak to my father, and even my cousin Percival if necessary." His face darkened. "We believe that my mother's letters may never have been given to my father by him as he assured me while I was in prison, and Adam is going to confront Beth."

Beth again. A pang stabbed through Elizabeth.

She stared at him and then pushed away the sharp taste of jealousy. He had never loved Beth. Then suddenly she realized what it meant. Joy flooded through her and she beamed at him. "Oh, John, he's going to prove your innocence!"

Her hands went out to him of their own volition. An answering gleam of excitement shone on his face as he grasped them tightly and drew her closer.

"He says that if he can prove that I am the legitimate heir to a peerage, my trial would be proved invalid and I would have to be tried by my peers. Oh, Elizabeth, how I have longed to see you, to tell you. . ."

And then their arms were around each other and they were clinging together. He looked into her bright eyes and groaned helplessly as his lips descended to plunder hers.

Mrs. Richmond entered the room and stopped dead. "Elizabeth!"

They sprang apart guiltily, but Elizabeth refused to let go of his hand as she turned to her friend. "Oh, Mrs. Richmond, Adam's going to see John's father to prove his innocence."

Mrs. Richmond looked from one to the other and shook her head helplessly. During one bad patch the previous year when Elizabeth had sobbed out her grief and loneliness onto her friend's shoulder, she had repeated to Mrs. Richmond all that John had told her. She had told Elizabeth today that after telling her husband he had said, "In no way must you encourage her in those wild fantasies, my dear."

Now she sighed and moved slowly forward to touch Elizabeth's flushed cheek lightly. "My dear, this is the first day since being told about your father, that you have that old happy gleam back in your eyes." She looked up at John. There was censure in her direct look but she merely said, "I do wish you all the best, Mr. Martin," and then gave them both a smile that to her credit only wavered for a moment.

"I earnestly hope Adam succeeds, my dear," she said gently to Elizabeth as she moved forward and took her hand so that she was forced to relinquish her grip on John's hand. "But I would urge you both not to get your hopes up too much."

ten

Despite an occasional tense moment between John and Elizabeth, the three of them had a most enjoyable evening. The two women were fascinated by the stories John told about Adam's sheep station. Both knew the difficulties of farming on the fertile Bathurst plains, but this country west of the Macquarie River and the small settlement at Wellington was something different again.

"When the explorer Captain Charles Sturt returned from exploring the Castlereagh and Bogan River areas out there only a couple years before Father sent me to England, he told about a large and sun-blasted plain with little vegetation," Elizabeth said eagerly. "Have you found there is sufficient pasture for the sheep?"

For a moment, John was caught by staring into her excited, flashing eyes and lost his train of thought. Then the color rose in her cheeks, and Mrs. Richmond coughed delicately. John glanced swiftly at her. She was looking at Elizabeth with some astonishment and then caught his eyes.

To his considerable relief Mrs. Richmond suddenly beamed at him ap-provingly and said, "Do tell us what the country is like, John."

He smiled back at her and relaxed even more. "I believe where we are is not quite as arid as further west, but this time of the year it is very hot."

The time flew by as he went on to tell them about the discovery that the size of the block of land Adam had leased was proving to be inadequate. The pastures could not sustain the same number of sheep per acre as the more eastern properties, and they were being forced to occupy a much larger area than expected to find enough grass for the sheep.

"That's been happening all over the country for many years," Mrs. Richmond said comfortably. "It was only last year that we were allowed to buy licenses to pasture stock beyond the authorized limit."

Elizabeth grinned happily at her but eagerly turned back to John as he went on to tell them about the huge mobs of kangaroos that also competed with the sheep for the grass.

"And you've had some contact with the aboriginals, John," Elizabeth noted anxiously. "Are they dangerous?"

"The aboriginals in the area had never seen white men before," John told them. "They are quite friendly, although very suspicious, and keep to themselves. They started helping themselves to several sheep not long after we arrived. We never saw them, and most of the men were scared and all for going after them, but Adam managed to make contact and eventually befriend them. He is a great man," he added, and they heard in his voice how much he had grown to love him.

He went on to tell them how Adam had managed to set up a system where he let the aboriginals have a sheep every now and again as well as some flour and sugar, on condition they would not disturb the flocks. He had also promised not to venture on certain land that they seemed to hold as taboo or used for their huge *corroborees*.

He had insisted all his workmen treat them and their women with respect and dignity. So far there had not been as many problems with them as there had been in other areas where the white man had intruded on the aboriginal territory.

Then some of the sheep had lambed just as the worst of the freezing westerly winds had swept in, and there had been more losses than they had hoped. But on the whole, Adam had not been too displeased with their first cut and the bales of wool that had been hauled away by their bullock teams a couple months ago.

"Have you. . .have you been very lonely way out there, John?" Elizabeth asked softly at one point.

He looked at her for a long moment, and she saw the

answer in his eyes before he looked down.

"Yes, there were times I was lonely," he murmured at last, "but somehow lately it hasn't been too bad. There's a special charm about the country that I can't really explain." He smiled wryly. "A sense of absolute freedom is certainly perhaps its biggest attraction, but there is a timelessness about the land that so often puts life into its right perspective. I have felt very close to God out there on the flat plains as well as in the silence of the bush."

No one spoke for a few moments, and then John looked directly at Elizabeth and said quietly, "Your father must have been a great man. Adam told us just before he sailed that your father had given him those sheep and his rights to that property."

"Apparently my father had obtained that land just before he was killed. All the plans had been made and most of the provisions already organized. I'm just so glad he left it to Adam," Elizabeth told him proudly. "It was no real surprise to me. Before I went to England he told me he was making provision for Adam in his will. Adam had saved his life more than once. . ." Her face clouded.

"And he would have again, if it had been in his power," Mrs. Richmond said briskly. She suddenly stood up. "I'm afraid my husband may be home soon. I know that he will want to speak to you, Mr. Martin, but perhaps it would be best if you called in the morning?"

As he too rose to his feet, John looked at her steadily. He understood her silent message that it would be best if that particular interview took place when Elizabeth was not present.

"Of course, madam," he said quietly, "I must apologize if I have outstayed my welcome."

A hint of color touched the older woman's face, but she merely nodded and graciously allowed him to take her hand as he bowed his farewell. "Perhaps you would like to see Mr. Martin out, Elizabeth?" she relented enough to say.

Elizabeth slowly led the way to the front door and out onto the small front porch. She turned suddenly toward him and asked, "When were you intending to return to the station, John?"

"We promised Adam we would return as soon as possible." He smiled at her as she looked up at him with a slight frown. As though unable to resist touching her, he reached out and placed a finger on the creased, velvety skin of her forehead. "The men Adam has surrounded himself with know their jobs and seem pretty reliable, but I know Timothy is eager to show his wife and son the new house we have been working on."

Elizabeth thought of some of the settlers' rough bush cabins she had seen made of logs, bark, and mud, and shuddered. She hoped Mrs. Hardy was not too shocked by the primitive conditions.

"And are you sure you will both be all right while Adam is gone? Did he say how long he would be away?"

"He anticipated his business with his brother would be very brief. Apparently they have never got on, especially since his brother's marriage. He hoped to be well and truly back within twelve months, depending on his securing a passage home."

He gave a light laugh. "Adam made sure that Timothy's ticket-of-leave was renewed before he left and that my assignment to him was also endorsed while he was away. We both have all the documentation quite safely, including any passes he thought I might need to move from one district to another."

A sudden inexplicable sense of foreboding touched Elizabeth, and she reached out and clasped his hand. "You will be very careful, won't you John?" She hesitated and then said boldly, "I really think it would be safer for you all if I accompanied you on the journey west."

He looked silently at her for a moment and then turned away and clutched at the rail near the steps while he stared out across the front yard. *Accompany them to the outback!* There was nothing more he could have desired at that moment than her continued presence in his life, but he closed his eyes briefly in despair. She was so precious to him, and it was up to him to protect her.

He turned and looked at her sweet face raised so trustingly to his. "I must apologize for putting you in such an embarrassing situation earlier when Mrs. Richmond entered the room," he managed to say at last when he knew he had control of his voice and face.

Her smile dimmed slightly, but she said mischievously, "I'm not a bit sorry. I. . ." She took a deep breath. "I had hoped you might repeat it."

Because he could not help himself his hands went out to her. She clasped them firmly in her dainty ones and he clung to her while he searched her face in the dim glow from the outside lighting.

"Elizabeth, you know we can't do this," he said desperately.

She just smiled at him with so much love and gentleness in her face that his good intentions began to weaken. So desperately had he longed to see that smile, breathe that fragrance that always surrounded her, was the very essence of her.

"I know nothing of the sort," she said crossly, "whether you take me with you or not, I'm still coming. Besides, it would be much safer for me and my maid traveling with you than by ourselves," she said.

He guessed shrewdly that she would have had others with them on their journey, but refrained from comment when he saw the stubborn tilt of her chin. Suddenly he knew he was lost and started to smile at her.

Her eyes shone even brighter. "You. . .you shouldn't smile at me like that," she said a little breathlessly. "It does strange things to me. It always has."

He smiled in sudden delight. *It was nothing to what her smile did to him!*

"Can you possibly be ready by tomorrow though?" he said doubtfully. "We have already been here longer than we had thought because the *Royal Admiral* was delayed, and we can't really afford to stay at the inn any longer."

"Tomorrow!" She looked taken aback, but then smiled a little grimly. "No doubt it is just as well. I should imagine I will be glad to get away from the Richmonds and their lectures."

His doubt and dismay increased. Before he could open his mouth to again argue against her going, she lifted her chin and added hurriedly, "Of course I can be ready, but you did say you would call on Dr. Richmond in the morning."

He hesitated for a long moment and then sighed. *So be it.*

His grip on her hand tightened. "Timothy wanted to show his wife and son a little of Sydney before we leave. I will come here instead of joining them. We thought we would have an early lunch before we head off and camp just this side of the pass through the Blue Mountains tonight. Then a full day tomorrow should bring us well on our journey. We will travel much faster on the last stretch than our first time," he mused.

She stared up at him with such starry eyes that John felt his heart swell and could no longer resist. He swept her into his arms and eagerly claimed the lips she raised willingly to him.

"Twelve months ago I determined this could never happen again," he murmured against her lips and then gave a soft moan as her hands tightened and he kissed her again.

They were both breathless when they at last drew a little apart and stared at each other in wonder.

"Elizabeth, you do know there is so much I am longing to say to you, but I cannot, I must not! Not while I am a convicted felon."

Elizabeth felt in a daze. The words seemed to burst from him, and she lifted a dainty hand and placed it firmly over his lips. He grasped it and held the palm to his lips.

"I know, John, I know. But surely you can tell me one thing. Do you. . ." She paused, remembering all the etiquette her poor aunt had tried to drill in her for dealing with members of the opposite sex.

So what? Surely it wasn't "etiquette" to kiss a convict either!

She raised her head and said steadily, "I love you, John Martin, but I know any chance of our relationship going further depends on what Adam can accomplish in England."

She felt the strong, muscular body so close to hers tremble as he stared at her. A myriad of expressions chased themselves across his face. She thought she saw love and hope. . .and then doubt.

Doubt? Doubt of Adam's success? Doubt of her love for him? Or doubt about his own feelings for her?

The thought slammed into her and she stepped back, searching his face. After all, there had been someone else in England for him. Beth.

She slowly drew in a deep breath, knowing she had to ask the question that had been haunting her.

"It also depends on how much you. . .you love me and also your. . .your feelings about Beth. Do you still. . ." She gulped and finished in a rush. "Are your feelings for Beth still there in any way at all? If—when—you are proven innocent, will you want to see her again?"

"Beth?" Sheer amazement stared at her from his dark eyes. Then he frowned savagely. "My friendship with her could have perhaps grown into something deeper, but any chance of that died completely when she did not answer any of my letters after I had been arrested and then did not come to the trial."

Relief swept through Elizabeth.

"Oh, Elizabeth, Beth was certainly pretty and gentle, the first person I had met in England who seemed to really care about me, who offered me real friendship. Because of my accent and being a foreigner, everyone else treated me with some measure of suspicion. I was lonely, and I think for some reason she was going through a very rebellious stage," he finished slowly.

Elizabeth withdrew her hands from his and clenched them so tightly her nails cut into her palms. "And can you be sure what you feel for me is not caused from the same reasons?" she asked quietly.

He stared at her silently for a long moment. Then he lifted one finger and traced it so tenderly down her face that she shivered.

"Beth and I only knew each other properly a few weeks, whereas you and I lived in close proximity for months. Besides, Timothy and Adam are my very good friends now, so with my relationship with God, I'm no longer alone like I was then, even out in the isolation of the outback. I've known you much longer, and the way I feel about you cannot begin to compare with my feelings for her."

She searched his face, wanting desperately to believe him. "But you haven't told me yet what those feelings are, John."

As though shutting out her irresistible, pleading face, he closed his eyes tightly. "Oh, Elizabeth, can't you see that until I am free I dare not? There is no future for us unless Adam succeeds with his efforts on my behalf!"

Then they stared at each other. Sudden fear pierced through Elizabeth, and with a low murmur of distress she reached out to him again. "And while we wait, John?"

John looked at her, aching to tell her how desperately he loved her. He drew on every ounce of strength and faith he had and said steadily, "We will pray and trust in God. We will remember that He is good, and His goodness, His keeping power never fails."

Then he drew her into his arms again, and they held each other close for another delicious moment before Elizabeth slowly pulled away and stared earnestly up at him. "So you do really believe," she marveled, "even after all you have been through."

He nodded. "More and more each day," he said briefly, and she looked down.

"It's been so hard, so very hard for me to keep on believing, trusting in God this past year," she confessed in a small voice. "Ever since your. . .that bad time on board ship, I have been full of doubts. I prayed so hard God would stop it, and when He didn't. . . There have been many times since when I have doubted God's love, His care. . ."

John took a deep breath. "When I feel like that—and Timothy assures me it is perfectly all right to doubt as long as we work through those times—those are the occasions I spend reading about the cross," he said in a whisper. "That's where we know beyond a shadow of a doubt that God loves and cares."

She searched his eyes longingly. "I do so long to have fellowship with you and Timothy again in spiritual things," she said so wistfully that he gave a low, delighted laugh and bent for one more swift kiss.

"It will happen, my dear Elizabeth, it will happen. Starting tomorrow, it will happen."

Then he turned reluctantly away before he weakened any further. With a determined set to his shoulders, he walked out into the night.

When he reached the first curve in the long driveway from the main road to the house, he looked back and waved one more time toward the outline of her figure in the light of the doorway. He saw her hand lift, and then she was gone.

Tomorrow. Tomorrow he would see her again. Would be traveling with her for days.

He took a deep breath of sheer joy, and there was a spring in his step as he strode away.

Fortunately the Richmonds' house was no great distance from the inn. He was not sorry he had refused Mrs. Richmond's polite offer of a coach even for that relatively short distance. He needed time to think, to ponder on all they had said, and what he had longed to say. His heart beat with wonder, but it also ached.

How he had longed to tell Elizabeth how precious she was to him. How he longed to be able to ask her to be his wife. Tonight at least he had been strong enough, but what about tomorrow and the days after that? Doubt slowed his steps. Was she wise to return with them? Of course not. But he doubted now if he could stop her.

A rustling in the bushes brought his thoughts back to his surroundings. He suddenly realized he had forgotten just how far it was along this drive to the main thoroughfare. It had still been light when he had arrived, and now, away from the entrance lights of the house, it was very dark.

He had spent many hours on the open plains after the sun had set, but for some reason the trees and low scrub pressing close to the edge of the single carriageway seemed menacing.

As his footsteps rang on the hard, rough stones, he shook his head at himself with a slight smile, but hastened his stride. There came another rustling in the bushes. He thought he heard a step behind him and paused briefly to glance around.

There was no one there, but a strange sense of uneasiness crept over him along with the certainty that he was not alone. There were two-legged creatures of the night who preyed on others. He hastened his steps even more, only to stop dead as he turned a corner and a large figure moved from the shadows and loomed just in front of him.

"Well, well," a sneering voice said loudly, "what do we have here? If it isn't that fellow Martin!"

John froze. This was no common footpad. He recognized that high-pitched voice.

"Edwards?" He managed to keep his voice steady but glanced quickly behind him. His heart sank as two men walked from behind some nearby trees and advanced quickly. One was much taller than the other, but a gleam of moonlight flashed on steel in the smaller man's hand.

"Now what would a scum convict be doing out here, do you suppose, gentlemen?"

"Going about his lawful business," John said calmly, while his heart started to pound. He glanced quickly to both sides, wondering at his chance of giving them the slip.

Cecil Edwards gave a bray of laughter. "Lawful! Lawful, you say?"

He moved closer, and John's heart sank as he saw the pistol in his clenched fist. "I have all the papers I need to be allowed abroad," he said sharply.

"Do you now? Papers can go missing, Martin, but I'm so glad you informed me of that."

There was deadly menace in the rapid words. John's heart

became a block of ice. The man intended to destroy his papers and haul him before a magistrate as an escaped convict. Any assigned convict moving out of his immediate area for any reason at all needed signed passes on him at all times. With Adam overseas, it would be nigh to impossible to prove that his master had written and signed such papers.

No. He was wrong. This man would not risk Dr. Richmond's interference again. He intended to kill him now as a convict trying to escape being apprehended. Being so far from his master's property with no passes on him would be all that was needed for Edwards to escape punishment.

There was another loud, mocking laugh. "What do you think, men? I'd say there's nothing lawful about a convict being out after dark." He paused, seeming to consider, then said with another sneer, "Unless of course there was a skirt involved."

John tensed even more. "You've been following me," he said flatly.

Now he knew for sure this was a premeditated attack, an ambush. Sergeant Hobbs had been right to warn him, but he had thought that with Edwards safely in Van Dieman's Land and after all this time. . .

He drew in a deep breath.

"Ever since I saw you meet up with our mutual friend on the wharf this morning, I've had you followed," the triumphant voice told him. "And how is our charming Miss Waverley?"

John thought rapidly, his eyes trying to pierce the darkness to find a way of escape. But suddenly the three men rushed him at once, and after a brief struggle he was held fast with the pistol held hard against his head. For a moment he thought it was the end and offered up a brief prayer.

Then the pistol was removed. A sharp command was given, and rough hands were searching his coat. His heart sank even farther as his pouch was found and its contents withdrawn.

"Well, well, what do we have here," Edwards crowed. *"Tut,*

tut, I'm sure these papers must have been stolen. Can be of no value at all."

John watched helplessly as a match suddenly flared. Soon the precious papers that guaranteed him safe passage were blazing brightly. In the brief light he saw that both men holding him were watching the fire. He thought he saw a brief flash of sympathy as the larger man looked from the burning papers toward him.

Suddenly, with some relief he knew these were not soldiers out of uniform as he had feared. They were probably convicts themselves or ex-convicts that Lieutenant Edwards had coerced or even paid to assist him. He had learned very quickly there was a special bond between convicts and ex-cons.

❧

He made up his mind swiftly and drawled insolently, "I thought you had been transferred to Van Dieman's Land. Were you too brutal for even that dreadful place? What happened, Lieutenant—or should I say Sergeant Edwards? I heard you were demoted for your unjust flogging and barbaric treatment of us aboard the *Royal Lady*."

As John had hoped, the men holding him loosened their hold somewhat and gaped at him. Obviously this was news to them. Then they looked uncertainly towards Edwards.

"You wouldn't be that Floggin' Sergeant Edwards that flogged me old mate to death a few months ago in Port Arthur just before I finished me time here, would you?" the tall man snarled suddenly.

Edwards laughed harshly. "And who would that be, do you suppose? There's been many a flogging of scum who needed to be reminded who was master."

The words had hardly left his lips when John felt the large man's hands let him go as he took a step towards Edwards. With a swift movement John brought his boot down on the other man's foot and slammed his elbow savagely into his ribs.

Even as his old enemy gave a howl of rage, John twisted away. He sprang swiftly to his right and made for the shelter offered by the dark shadows of the bush.

The men behind him hesitated for a moment, but Edwards screamed, "Get him! I'll double the money if you don't let him get away!"

They rushed after him. The smaller one flung something that for a brief moment caught a moonbeam on its blade. The knife caught John on his shoulder just as he leaped wildly across the wide ditch he had noticed beside the track.

There were loud curses behind him, and he knew his ploy had worked. They had blundered into the ditch. But it would not delay them long, and he had been cut enough for his shoulder to be aching badly. He felt a warm trickle down his arm as he tried to glide as swiftly and as quietly as he could through the trees, thankful for the many lessons the aboriginals he had befriended had taught him about moving swiftly and silently when hunting.

After some time, he managed to elude them enough to at last scramble up a tall tree and hide among its branches. He listened to the sound of his pursuers fading away. Then his head sank down onto his arms in near despair.

He knew beyond doubt that with his papers gone, Edwards would successfully post him as an escaped convict. He could be shot on sight, well before Dr. Richmond or Elizabeth could intervene. Even aboriginals often caught escaped convicts and dragged them back to their masters or to the soldiers. Some desperate men ended up as bushrangers, terrorizing travelers and isolated settlers.

Briefly he thought of making his way back to the Richmonds' house. After a few moments he shook his head. He was not sure where he was, only that he had run a long way into the bush. By the time he found the house, Edwards would probably already be watching it again. He'd no doubt also have someone watching the inn.

John sucked in a shuddering breath. Would the man, as crazy as he seemed to be, try to harm Timothy? Then he remembered the rage in Edwards' eyes on board the ship when he had looked from Elizabeth to himself. She had dared to favor a convict over and above the smart, successful lieutenant. After all, he had let Timothy off the lash even if it had been really an excuse to give John more punishment.

He shuddered. He very much doubted if Edwards would bother with the other man. But knowing Timothy, he could get caught up in any fight that threatened his friend and risk losing his ticket-of-leave. It wasn't worth that risk.

And that left Dr. Richmond. The man had been just and fair to his charges on board ship, and yet he had deliberately gone to considerable lengths to protect Elizabeth from any more contact with him.

In so many ways, he agreed that it was right that Dr. Richmond should try to protect his old friend's daughter, even more so when her only relatives lived a world away in England. John doubted very much if Dr. Richmond would want to help him again, especially after his wife told him what she had interrupted this evening.

Somehow he had to stay out of Edwards' clutches until Adam returned.

There was only one thing he knew he could do.

eleven

After waving to John one last time, Elizabeth slowly entered the house. She hesitated for a moment, knowing she should join her hostess again in the drawing room. Instead, she turned and flew to her bedroom to pace and dwell on every word John had said. She half-expected Mrs. Richmond would follow her but was thankful when no knock came.

It had been a long time since she had attended a church service or even prayed, but suddenly she flung herself on her knees. "Oh, God, You've been watching out for John after all. I do thank You!"

Her voice was choked with tears as she thought of all the dangers he had been through. As she opened her heart again to God, the words tumbled out. She poured out all her personal anguish and doubts. After a long time peace came and that sense of warmth and love from God that she had been missing for a long time.

"I'm so sorry, Lord," she whispered at last. "I've been forgetting about You. Please help me to be stronger, more faithful. It's so hard out there so far from Christian fellowship. Help me to trust You all the time, and oh, show me what I must do," she burst out.

A few tears were shed, but then she sat and thought for a long time.

Then she started making plans.

When she did at last climb into bed, Elizabeth was too excited to sleep very well and was up early. The woman servant she had brought with her was not averse to packing and returning home immediately.

"Don't like the city no more," the woman born and bred in the bush said with such a relieved look on her face that

Elizabeth laughed out loud in understanding and sympathy.

But as she made her way at last to the breakfast room, she braced herself. As fond as her friends were of their property in the country, she knew they did not share her love of the life. And as for returning with John. . .

She took a deep breath and entered the room. Dr. Richmond and his wife were already seated at the table, talking in low voices. They looked up as she entered, and her heart sank at their grave faces.

They became even more distressed when she told them bluntly she was returning with John and Timothy. "I want them to see Waverley Station and stay for a brief visit if they possibly can, and then I would like to accompany them to Stevens Downs," she added firmly.

"Elizabeth, surely you cannot have thought this through. There just cannot be any future for you with a man serving a life sentence!" Dr. Richmond exploded at last.

Elizabeth could not refrain from looking at her friend with reproach.

"Of course Mrs. Richmond told me about the man having the nerve, the effrontery to kiss you!" he added, correctly interpreting their exchange of glances.

Elizabeth grinned happily. "I do believe it may have been me who actually had the effrontery to kiss him. He is filled with the same foolish scruples you have, sir."

She put her head mischievously on one side. "But then," she added thoughtfully, "I'm not absolutely positive who started to kiss whom, but I think it must have been me, because John was almost as concerned as you about it afterward."

"Elizabeth!"

Mrs. Richmond's rather shocked exclamation barely registered. Elizabeth was thinking of that kiss. Despite his concern, it had not stopped John from kissing her again later. The jubilant thought and the memory that accompanied it brought the heat to her cheeks. Mrs. Richmond was studying her thoughtfully, and Elizabeth had the uncomfortable feeling she knew about those other kisses as well.

To Elizabeth's immense relief, Mrs. Richmond's lips started to twitch but she looked quickly down to hide her face. With renewed confidence she answered all Dr. Richmond's arguments with a smile until he at last stopped and shook his head sadly at her.

"There's nothing I can say to change your mind, is there?"

Elizabeth smiled at him gently. "I love John Martin and if as my guardian you will not give me permission to marry him, then I will wait until I am of age."

She paused then and looked down at her hands. "But you may not have to worry," she added softly. "He has not even asked me to marry him yet." Her smile disappeared as she faced the truth. "And he will never ask me to marry him unless he can prove his innocence."

Sudden relief filled Dr. Richmond's face. "Then he is a man worthy of your love after all."

To Elizabeth's astonishment, Mrs. Richmond sprang to her feet. "Oh, my dear Elizabeth, I can't bear that deep anguish and hurt in you. I have seen it every time we have met these last twelve months, and I've known it wasn't only because of your poor father's death."

She turned on her husband. "You men are all alike," she spat out, "you think only of the noble, the honorable thing. No matter that we women break our hearts while knowing what is best for us!"

He murmured a startled disclaimer, and Elizabeth stared open-mouthed at her friend. Not once had she ever heard her speak so to her husband.

"I saw in these two young people yesterday such love that I know is very rare. There was no doubting that young man's love for you, Elizabeth. He was suffering terribly because he could not confess that love openly. And you. . ."

She stopped, her voice wavering, and Elizabeth saw tears form in her eyes. "Can't you see the change in her this morning? You know as well as I that she has not been able to mention her father, but last night she did so naturally to John Martin. It's as though all these months she's been making all the outward motions of living, but look at the light in her face. She's alive again, and that man is responsible!"

She turned and strode over to Elizabeth and enveloped her in a huge, slightly tearful hug. "If he doesn't ask you to marry him, you ask him, Elizabeth Waverley—and don't take no for an answer. Men!"

"Agnes!"

Both women ignored the shocked doctor as they hugged each other.

"Excuse me, ma'am, this man said he had to see someone."

All three turned toward the doorway and the worried voice. Mrs. Richmond's new serving woman was wringing her hands nervously. Suddenly Timothy Hardy appeared behind her and strode into the room.

Elizabeth sprang to her feet. "Why Timothy, what—"

"Is John still here?"

She put one hand to her lips to stifle her cry of dismay. Something had seriously upset the usually placid little man. It was Dr. Richmond who answered him.

"As you can see, Mr. Hardy, your friend is not here. Now, may we please hear your reason for bursting—"

"He didn't return to the inn last night, and I just found these on the road." He held out a handful of charred remnants of paper. "They look very much like John's passes."

Elizabeth looked wildly from one man to the other as Dr. Richmond examined the scraps of paper. "Something's happened to him," she whispered. "He was going straight back to the inn."

"That's what I fear, Miss Waverley. And there's something else. My wife told me the *Royal Admiral* called at Van Dieman's Land on the way here. That's why they were late arriving. A Sergeant Edwards joined them for the trip to Sydney."

Mrs. Richmond gave a distressed cry. Her husband said

grimly, "I heard only yesterday that he had been transferred back here. I meant to warn you all this morning. We must start a search for Mr. Martin immediately."

Elizabeth desperately wanted to join the searchers that were quickly organized. She only agreed to stay home when Mrs. Richmond said, "I think you should stay with me. Perhaps John may be trying to find his way back here."

She glanced up at her husband's stern face as she spoke, and Elizabeth saw the glance they exchanged. "You don't hold out much hope of finding him, do you?" she asked dully.

Dr. Richmond finished pulling on his coat and said gently, "We can only pray he has gotten away from that evil man, Elizabeth, but without those papers on him, he is in grave danger. The mere fact he has not returned here if he was attacked is cause for concern."

After he had gone, his wife said thoughtfully, "I'm not sure if he would return here. He was apprehensive about speaking to Dr. Richmond and may have doubted whether he would help him."

"He would be more concerned about involving me," Elizabeth said flatly, "probably the same reason he did not go to the inn—because he wouldn't want to involve Timothy. Supposing of course that. . .that. . ." Her voice broke.

"Now, no thinking like that," Mrs. Richmond said sharply, "Timothy told us he searched the immediate area on both sides of the track where he found the burnt papers. It looked as though there had been a scuffle and signs that more than one person had forced a way through the bush. It's far more likely he managed to get away. He may be still hiding or even have become lost out there."

But a grim-faced search party returned several hours later.

"We followed the trail for quite some distance into the bush, but then we lost it," an exhausted Dr. Richmond reported to the two women as he marched up the front steps.

Elizabeth swayed and clung to a verandah post.

"One thing you may be sure of then," Mrs. Richmond said

swiftly with a warning look at her husband. "Whatever happened, it would appear that John managed to get away."

There was a sudden sound of clattering hoofbeats. They swung around as a detachment of uniformed men swung into sight.

Elizabeth gasped as she recognized the man leading them.

"Careful now, ladies," Dr. Richmond said softly. "Leave this to me."

Fierce anger burned in Elizabeth as Cecil Edwards bowed mockingly toward them from his saddle. "Dr. Richmond. Ladies."

Dr. Richmond had moved swiftly and left the house to confront the men in the yard. With his hands on his hips he asked sharply, "What do you want, Edwards?"

The man's eyes widened, and he said maliciously, "An escaped convict." He relished hearing Elizabeth's small gasp, and his eyes mocked her as he added, "An old friend of yours, I believe, Miss Waverley. Mr. John Martin has been seen in this city far away from his assigned master's property, and, when confronted, ran into the bush. I have informed the magistrates, and he has been posted as an absconded convict."

Mrs. Richmond's warning touch on Elizabeth's arm was all that stopped her from racing down the steps and physically attacking the scoundrel. It was all so reminiscent of another place, another time when John's life had been in danger from this horrible man.

"And what makes you search for him here, sir?" Dr. Richmond asked angrily.

Edwards' eyes glinted. "Why, he was last seen leaving this very house, my dear Doctor. Is it not natural that we should commence our search and enquiries here?"

"I can assure you he is not here." Dr. Richmond's scornful glance raked over all the mounted men. They lingered for a moment on one man not in uniform. He raised his voice. "I would strongly advise you to commence your search elsewhere and make sure you treat this man fairly when you capture him or you will have me to deal with."

Elizabeth relaxed slightly as the soldiers stirred restlessly and watched their leader. All obviously knew of the influence Dr. Richmond held.

Cecil Edwards suddenly lost his false affability. "Oh, we'll find him. You can be sure of that. Dead or alive, we'll find him, and if it is in my power it will be dead!"

No one moved until the horsemen had disappeared in a cloud of dust as quickly as they had come.

Slowly Dr. Richmond turned and joined the two women. Angry tears blurred Elizabeth's vision, but she brushed them aside and stared at him as she heard him give a sudden laugh and say, "Well, that is a relief, my dears."

He saw her bewilderment and said quickly, "Don't you see? It is obvious that Edwards has most certainly had something to do with John's disappearance and those burnt papers, but somehow John has managed to elude him." He hesitated and then added, "I did not want to distress you further by telling you that Timothy found a trail of blood before he came here this morning. We were afraid. . ."

He broke off and Elizabeth said slowly, "You thought he might already have been killed?"

Dr. Richmond nodded abruptly. "But don't you see, if he was dead, Edwards would be gloating, not mounting a search. And don't be mistaken, he was one very angry and frustrated man!"

Elizabeth stared at him, suddenly filled with hope. "And I think I know where John will be heading," she said slowly, and then flung around and gave Mrs. Richmond a swift hug. "Timothy and I must leave immediately."

She looked up and saw Timothy Hardy watching them from the open doorway. "Oh, Timothy, what do you think? Do you think John will try and make his way back to Stevens Downs?"

He hesitated, his face stern. "I heard what was said, but I thought it best if that man did not know I was here. The only place John would be safe until Adam returns would be back on the property where he was assigned to work." He paused, and then added grimly, "But if we know that, so does Lieutenant Edwards, and he will be after him."

"Then Elizabeth is right, and there is no time to lose." Mrs. Richmond bustled forward. "I hope your things are packed, my dear. It should not take me long to do my own."

"Agnes!"

She rounded on her husband and glared at him. "Walter, you do not think for one moment I am going to allow this child to go into all kinds of dangers in a strange place without my support, do you?"

Dr. Richmond looked at her helplessly. "But my dear, you know I cannot accompany you at such short notice. There are patients relying on me, and I must be here when the news arrives from London."

Elizabeth exchanged a glance with Timothy, and with one accord they turned and entered the house, leaving the husband and wife to fight it out between them.

❧

Elizabeth had long since said good-bye to Timothy, with the promise of being at the inn as soon as possible, before Mrs. Richmond rejoined her. Her friend's face was solemn, her eyes gleaming with so much excitement, Elizabeth refrained from complaining at her tardiness.

"Elizabeth, I have decided it is much better if we delay leaving until at least tomorrow."

She opened her mouth for a sharp retort, but Mrs. Richmond raised her hand and said forcefully, "I have promised Dr. Richmond faithfully not to say a word, but do believe me when I say it is essential that we give him time to put a couple things in place before we head west. He says he may even be able to organize joining us in a few days."

Mrs. Richmond gave an excited laugh. "Oh, my dear, he really does only have your interest at heart and has come up with the most marvelous scheme. Indeed, I am sorry I promised not to reveal what he is planning, but I did, and you must trust us."

"I trusted you twelve months ago," Elizabeth said challengingly after studying her friend's smiling face for a long moment. "Why should I now?"

Mrs. Richmond's smile disappeared. "We are both truly sorry, Elizabeth, for the way we deceived you. After he returned last night and then again this morning, Dr. Richmond and I discussed everything that has happened in considerable depth. He agrees with me now that in our desire to protect you we made a grave error of judgment."

She hesitated and then added swiftly, "Adam has sent us very regular reports about John Martin these past twelve months. He has had nothing but praise for the man. He also visited us before he left for England."

She smiled at Elizabeth's exclamation and said, "Yes, we already knew about him making some attempt to prove John's innocence. He also told us that he truly believes him to be innocent, and we had to admit that after what you both have told us, we also hold out high hopes that he will succeed."

Elizabeth stared at her. Then tears of relief started trickling down her face. "Oh, if only he does. He must."

After indulging in a few more tears she calmed down enough to say ruefully, "So I suppose that means we had better send a message to Timothy to delay our departure."

"No, not theirs, ours."

Elizabeth looked at her in some surprise.

"Timothy told Dr. Richmond that they have a couple heavy wagon loads containing supplies as well as his wife's things, so they will be traveling very slowly. It would be much better for them to camp somewhere on the road tonight, just in case Mr. Martin is waiting for them. If we travel light and leave tomorrow morning, we will have no problem catching up with them, probably before they have crossed the Blue Mountains. We'll send them a message to that effect."

But she was wrong. By evening the next day their carriage

had still not overtaken them. Timothy must have made better time than expected, and Elizabeth became concerned as they started down through the rolling hills on the western slopes of the Great Dividing Range.

They were traveling as light as they could and had made good time, despite a later start than she had hoped. All their luggage and camping equipment had been rushed over to the inn to accompany the Hardys. Dr. Richmond had also sent a couple of men with Timothy as well as sending some of his most trusted men with the three women.

But at last, just as the last rays of the sun were changing the sky to glorious shades of pink and gold, Elizabeth and Mrs. Richmond rounded a curve in the dusty road in their fast carriage and came up to the large wagons laden down with camping equipment, food, and building supplies.

"Mr. Hardy's taking his missus on ahead to set up camp," they were told by the two men handling the reins of the huge cart horses.

It wasn't long before a small figure suddenly appeared from behind the trunk of a majestic old gum tree and waved vigorously to them. "Miss Waverley, Miss Waverley, Father left me to show you the way!"

Elizabeth smiled wearily at young Tim's excited face and instructed one of their outriders to let him climb up behind him so he could show them the way.

A neat camp was in the throes of being set up in a grassy clearing amidst tall timber beside a small, swiftly flowing creek. A carefully prepared fire was already blazing cheerfully on the pebbles at the water's edge, with a blackened tin of water heating slowly.

Elizabeth looked quickly around, and her heart sank when no tall, black-haired man appeared. Timothy was studying their faces hopefully, and when Elizabeth shook her head, his face darkened.

His wife bustled forward. "No word yet of Mr. Martin, then? Well that means at least he is most likely to be still at large," he said comfortingly. "Now, you must be tired after coming so far so quickly. The water should be boiled soon, and then we can all have a nice cup of tea."

Elizabeth did not manage a quiet word with Timothy until later that evening. "Timothy," she began hesitantly, "you saw the blood stains. Do you think John could have been seriously injured?"

"Oh, no, Miss," he answered swiftly, "there were only a few smears of blood a little way into the bush, and then again later we found some on the bark of a tree as though he must have had some on his hand. I doubt very much if it he was hurt too badly."

Elizabeth relaxed a little. "Then why do you think he has not made contact with you? Surely he must know you would head straight for home."

"I thought he might be waiting for us last night." Timothy looked around at the shadows beyond the campfire that was slowly dying down. "But when he didn't turn up we got away at first light to make it here. This is where we stopped with Adam over twelve months ago. He told us then that it was a good place for camping overnight, and I hoped John would have remembered."

They were sitting on a large, flat rock near the water's edge. Elizabeth tossed a small twig into the water. They were silent for awhile, watching it drift slowly away, listening to the sounds of the bush all around them, the soft gurgles of the running water.

"How has he really been, Timothy?" Elizabeth asked softly after a long silence.

Timothy stirred restlessly. "He never forgets for a moment that he is a convict, or a government man as most of the other assigned convicts seem to prefer calling us."

She nodded with a slight smile and waited.

After a long moment, Timothy said quietly, "He still wakes up with nightmares at times."

Her heart clenched. "Night. . .nightmares?"

"He usually starts threshing around and mumbling, then h
might shout. Sometimes. . ." he hesitated and then adde
softly, "Sometimes he calls out your name."

Elizabeth turned her head swiftly towards him. "Does h
call 'Elizabeth' or 'Beth'?"

Timothy reached out a hand and touched her arm. "Eliza
beth," he said swiftly. "Never have I heard him mention Bet
since the night he told Adam all about what happened."

Warmth swept through her on a tide. "Oh, he has to be a
right, Timothy. He has had so much sadness in his life, so lit
tle love!"

"He will be," Timothy said fervently, "and even if he i
never acknowledged by his father, he will manage. Even if h
is never able to prove his innocence, he is a strong man an
he will cope. Besides, his trust in God has grown wonderfull
these past months."

Elizabeth smiled gratefully. They were both silent again
letting the peace of the bush settle their hearts.

"Did John tell you that Adam has been paying him as mucl
as he has me?"

Elizabeth shook her head. She knew that ticket-of-leav
men worked for wages, but except for their food and shelte
convicts did not have to be paid.

"It's not very much," Timothy continued, "but John ha
hardly touched his. Adam even bought our new clothes w
were wearing to meet the ship. John says that perhaps whe
he is free he will be able to have his own farm. He. . .he ofte
talks about when he'll be free."

Elizabeth was very tired but that night lay awake for hour
staring up at the stars. It was a very warm night, even thoug
they were still in the mountains, and she tossed and turned o
her hard makeshift bed of a blanket over leaves and branches

She wondered where John was. Had he found shelter? I
was comforting to know he must have a little money wit
him, but would he risk being recognized to buy some food?

"Oh, Lord, do watch over him tonight," she whispered

"and thank You that he knows You love and care for him."

Just when had she realized she loved John Martin? She thought back to that dirty, soaking wet convict who had risked his life to save young Tim. There had been something fine in the eyes that had searched hers intently, his anxiety for the boy showing in his cold, pale face.

Every contact she had with him after that had reinforced that deep inner knowledge that here was a special person, a wonderful man. And then he had shown his capacity for loving by taking Timothy's punishment that dreadful day.

Elizabeth shuddered, quickly banishing that particular horror as she had often done so many times before. John Martin was a man she was proud to love, and she would be even prouder if he loved her as passionately.

As she had the previous night in her soft bed at the Richmonds', she smiled as she thought of asking John to marry her. Then she wistfully hoped that she would never need to, that he would so honor her. She tried to remember if she had ever heard what a convict had to do to be allowed to marry. She knew that some men working for her father had been allowed to bring their wives to work on the station.

Wishing she had been brave enough to ask Dr. Richmond, she then wondered again, as she had several times, just what business he had insisted had been so important as to delay their journey. His wife had remained tight-lipped, just patting her hand and saying she had promised not to talk about it until the time was right.

Elizabeth dozed off and on but had fallen sound asleep when she was rudely awakened. The first faint streaks of dawn were lighting the sky and beginning to filter through the tall trees when three horsemen clattered into the center of their camp, shouting and cursing. At first she feared they were bushrangers, but then she recognized the voice she had hoped never to hear again.

Cecil Edwards shouted, "John Martin, we have you! Search thoroughly, men."

twelve

For one dreadful moment, Elizabeth froze. She looked wildly around at the piles of blankets near the wagons where the men had slept. *Had John arrived during the night?*

Timothy's voice rang out. "No one move or you will be shot!"

She swung around. Several of Dr. Richmond's men had appeared from behind the trees surrounding the campsite. Suddenly Elizabeth realized these men had been on watch all through the night. Their rifles were aimed directly at the three horsemen. Other men were scrambling from their bedrolls under the wagons and grabbing for their guns.

Edwards gave a furious oath and then shouted, "Are you going to impede an officer in the execution of his lawful duties? We are here to search for an escaped convict."

He kicked his horse forward. There was the sharp crack of a rifle. A puff of dirt rose from in front of him, and the horse shied violently, almost unseating its rider.

"But you will not be an officer very much longer, will you, Mr. Edwards?" a cool voice called out loudly.

Elizabeth stared at Mrs. Richmond. The rifle in her hand was pointed directly at Edwards.

"You have already been advised not to move, Mr. Edwards. My husband warned me you would follow us and this could happen. He also told me he discovered yesterday that charges are being prepared against you for excessive cruelty to prisoners in your care."

Elizabeth stared around numbly at the grim-faced men confronting Edwards and his two companions. Timothy was the only one who was not armed. Suddenly she realized why Dr. Richmond had sent so many of his men to accompany them as well as Timothy. Convicts and ticket-of-leave man were not allowed to bear arms. These were trusted servants, probably ex-military men, even emancipists.

"You won't be no soldier no more?"

Elizabeth looked sharply at the tall, rough-looking horseman who had flung the furious question at Edwards. She saw him look at his companion and then give a significant jerk of his head. They turned their horses.

"No money's worth bein' with you, Edwards. You've done naught but tell us lies since we agreed to help you," he shouted furiously as they moved away. "An' that you never flogged me mate must be another of them lies. We heard that the bloke who done it was likely to be kicked out of the army."

The circle of silent, grim-faced men moved and let the two men through. In a moment they had disappeared as quickly as they had come.

"I strongly suggest you go peacefully on your way, too, Mr. Edwards, and never break into someone's camp like this again," Mrs. Richmond said coldly. "We would have been justified thinking we were being raided by bushrangers and shooting you. Next time we might just do that."

In a moment the white-faced, defeated Edwards was swallowed up by the bush. No one moved until the noise of his going had ceased.

"Now perhaps John will be able to join us," Timothy said grimly, "but we'll still keep a look out for Edwards until we're back on Stevens Downs."

Was that why John had not shown up? Had he guessed that Edwards would undoubtedly follow Timothy or even herself? Elizabeth looked eagerly around, almost expecting him to step out of the bush. Then she forced a smile at Mrs. Richmond and shook her head at her friend. "You always manage to surprise me. I didn't realize you even knew how to shoot."

Mrs. Richmond snorted. "You forget that your mother and I were often left alone for long periods of time on our properties while our husbands were away. Both our husbands made very sure we knew how to use a gun."

The next few days, Elizabeth eagerly watched, but there was no sign of the man she loved. She knew Mrs. Richmond watched her anxiously and she usually managed to smile reassuringly at the older woman. But that smile became harder and harder to find late on the afternoon when they neared her home. The heavily laden wagons had made it a very slow journey. Long before this they had thought John would either be waiting for them or would have caught up. Confidence that he was still safe was at a very low ebb.

They were nearing the turnoff to Waverley Station when Elizabeth suddenly said to Mrs. Richmond, "I think we should send someone on to the homestead to see if he is there, but ourselves continue on to the Gordons' place."

"Why do you think John might go there and not to Waverley Station?"

"Why did he not return to your house?" Elizabeth answered her tartly. "The same reasons would send him to the Gordons'."

After a moment Elizabeth relented and said apologetically, "Apparently John has been there with Adam more than once this last year and been received very kindly. If he went anywhere, he would go there. Even though he now knows where my home is, none of my people know him."

She beckoned to Timothy, who was riding nearby. After she explained to him, he hesitated and then said, "From what you've told me, your place is closer. My Molly and young Tim are exhausted by the heat. Would you mind if I sent some of the other men with you and continued on with them?"

"Better still," Elizabeth said briskly, "why don't you let me have your horse? I can cut across country much faster. Mrs. Richmond is weary too and can accompany you up to the house. My people know her, where they would not recognize you."

Mrs. Richmond protested, "Why don't you just send a man over to the Gordons'?"

Elizabeth hesitated. How could she describe the burning

conviction she should go? She even wondered about it herself. *Was it God's direction or her own instinct?* At last she shrugged. "I don't know. I just feel I should go myself."

Mrs. Richmond stared at her, but at last merely said, "If you think you must, you must. But take a couple men with you."

Fortunately Elizabeth had dressed in a long, divided skirt that morning. Quickly she mounted astride Timothy's horse, and led the way swiftly through the scrub toward her neighbors'.

As they cantered at last up to her neighbors' long, low bush hut that housed their large family, it was almost dark. Anxiously Elizabeth looked around.

"Let's try the stables and barn first," she said briefly and led the way past the homestead to the cluster of buildings beyond it.

As they at last pulled to a stop, her neighbor strolled from the barn and waved to her. When she went to dismount, he held her horse and beamed at her. "Why, Miss Waverley, it has been a long time since your last visit."

She smiled wearily at him, but before she could speak, he grinned mischievously and drawled, "But somehow, I don't think it's us you have come to see this time either."

A soft voice from behind her said wonderingly, "Elizabeth?"

She swung around and stared unbelievingly at the tall figure that stood in the shadows of the stable.

"John? Oh, John, you're safe!" she cried out.

His arms opened instinctively and then closed around her as she hurled herself into them. She clasped him tightly, feeling again his strength, his tenderness, and then lifted her face and sighed as his lips closed passionately over hers.

"I've been so scared," she cried when she at last could speak. "How did you get here? We've been expecting to see you every day, every mile."

"I take it you know what happened," he said in a low voice. "And Timothy guessed I'd head for Stevens Downs, did he?"

"I think it was Dr. Richmond who first suggested it."

Elizabeth felt him stiffen. "Dr. Richmond?"

"Timothy found the charred remains of your papers and came to the house." Quickly she told him what had happened, including Cecil Edwards' appearance at their camp.

His face darkened. "So he is still chasing me." Then his expression changed again. "Did you say there were three of them?"

She nodded. "We haven't seen any sign of them since then, but we think he is so obsessed that he would not give up easily.

Then she was enfolded in his warm, strong arms again, and she was trembling and laughing even while the tears of relief flowed freely. "I was right, you are here. You're safe!"

"Well, blow me down, if this here geezer hasn't gone and got the prettiest girl in the west," a laughing voice exclaimed.

She had forgotten all about their audience, but when she turned quickly around, discovered to her relief that the men had taken the horses to unsaddle.

Blushing furiously, Elizabeth pulled away and beamed at Mr. Gordon. "Oh, sir, we have been so worried." She turned back to John and then cried out in distress.

He had moved out into the quickly fading light and she saw his face clearly for the first time. He was very pale, his clothes torn and filthy. Dark circles ringed his eyes, and even as she examined him he swayed.

He was looking at her with dazed eyes. "You are here, you are really here. I never expected. . ."

"Here man, come and sit down before you fall down." Will Gordon pushed past Elizabeth and grabbed hold of John as he swayed again. She, too, grabbed at his arm, but he winced and groaned and she let him go.

It was only then she saw the bloodstains on his shirt, and cried out, "Oh, John, you have been hurt!"

"Only arrived a few minutes before we saw your dust and knew someone was coming. He thought it might be the blokes what done this to him," Mr. Gordon said grimly, "so he stayed outta sight. Has only had time to tell us briefly someone's out to kill him. Destroyed his papers. He managed to get a ride in a bloke's carriage over the mountains and then bought an old nag. A couple of our men found him this afternoon on their rounds and brought him in. The old horse was nearly done."

All the time he had been firing his rapid words at Elizabeth, they were half-carrying John back into the barn. At last they set him down on a pile of fresh hay, and she anxiously crouched down beside him.

He managed to smile at her and gasped, "Just hungry and tired. Be all right soon."

"And hurt some." His shirt was already undone, and she pushed it back with trembling hands to expose his shoulder.

"Just got in the way of a knife. It's fine."

"Shush. Don't try and speak." Her hand lightly touched his cheek.

His hand came up and grabbed her wrist. "It was Edwards. I think he must be mad. Burnt my papers. Meant to kill me."

"Hush now," she soothed him. "We know. Don't try and talk just yet." She briefly told the other men about Cecil Edwards' visit to the house and then their camp.

Will Gordon scowled and muttered something under his breath she was glad she could not hear. "Right," he said sharply. "We'll keep a guard in case he is still following you, but be best to stay hidden here in the barn tonight just in case. Now, Miss, would you like to go up to the missus at the house, and—"

"No," Elizabeth said firmly, "I'm staying here with John. I'm not letting him out of my sight again," she added fiercely.

"Elizabeth," John began to protest but stopped when Mr. Gordon gave a hearty laugh.

"Still as stubborn as when you were a wee thing! Best not to argue, man. She'll not listen. We'll bring everything you and your lady need down to you from the house."

With that, he left them, and while they stared at each other, they heard him yelling out crisp orders. Elizabeth crept closer. John gave a huge sigh and with his good arm gathered her in.

They were silent for a long time, just content to be close. Explanations could wait until they had both rested and been cared for.

And cared for they were with the wonderful hospitality John had already discovered existed in the bush. Visitors were rare, and they were treated royally to food and hot water to refresh themselves and tend to John's wound. Clean clothes were even supplied for him.

By the time their needs had been met, it was night. The dark shadows were dispelled by a bright, full moon that beamed happily down. As much as Elizabeth would have liked to snuggle up beside John and share his rough bed of straw for the night, common sense prevailed when she saw her hostess's disapproving face at the briefest mention of it.

So reluctantly she let herself be led away to spotless linen and a comfortable bed in a room shared by a couple of shy, round-eyed children. The long, harrowing journey suddenly took its toll. She smiled at the children briefly before changing into borrowed nightclothes and tumbling into bed. She fell instantly into a deep sleep, not stirring until the sun was shining brightly.

"My goodness, child, you still look tired," Mrs. Gordon greeted her. "Do you really have to ride all the way over to your house today? I'm sure that young man needs to rest too. Why don't you stay awhile? I sure could do with another woman to talk to," she added so wistfully, that Elizabeth refrained from the hasty refusal already on her lips.

Elizabeth heard the sound of children laughing when she at last entered the barn. It seemed as though all but the two eldest Gordon children were crowded around John. Over their heads he smiled up at her so welcomingly and with so much love that for a moment a mist was before her eyes as she returned his quiet "good morning."

As she asked him about staying another day or so, she saw that John was already much better after a good sleep. He hesitated for a long moment, studying her intently. Then he gave one of his peculiar hand gestures and shrugs she always attributed to his Spanish upbringing. Then he nodded.

The children gave a whoop of delight, and then looked askance at her from their shy, dark eyes. She smiled gently back at them and was quite content to sit on an upturned bucket and watch with longing eyes John's interaction with them. As the children excitedly told him all about their lives since his last visit, he listened courteously, but his gaze often strayed to her.

He knew each of them by name, gently teasing them. He admired the various pets they brought to show him and listened intently to one long involved story about a large brown snake that their mother had killed in the hen enclosure only the day before.

It was obvious that he was very good with the children, especially with the quietest, shyest ones. She wondered about his cousins' children in Spain that he had told her about once during one of their rare times completely alone aboard ship. It had been obvious that he had loved them, despite their parents' antipathy towards him. Were they ever sad that he had disappeared from their lives?

What a wonderful father he would make, she found herself thinking, as he admired the yellow, fluffy little chicken the smallest child had presented him with. He stroked it with a gentle finger and looked up to give her one of his heart-shaking smiles.

She just looked at him.

The expression on his face changed. His eyes glowed like fire, and without taking his eyes from her, he said crisply, "All right, children, I need to speak with Miss Waverley for a while. Why don't you come back later? We might be able then to go and see that new foal you're all so excited about."

Neither of them moved for some time after the last child had reluctantly run from the barn.

"How come you look more beautiful every time I see you?" John said huskily at last.

The accent in his voice was suddenly very pronounced and

she looked up from her clasped hands, feeling suddenly shy and uncertain.

John saw the flush on her face and the expression in her eyes. His heart swelled. This beautiful woman loved him, really loved him. He took a deep breath and moved closer to her. He held out his hands. She did not move, just studied his face for a long moment.

He caught his breath, wondering what she could be thinking. Then a tremendous feeling of thankfulness filled him as he saw all her hesitancy vanish. Her face became so radiant that it nearly blinded him with her beauty. Then she was in his arms, and their lips met and told each other far more than mere words could ever have managed.

It was a magical day. Never before had they been so free to spend so much time at once together. For John it was bitter-sweet. He knew that soon they would once again be separated. *If only Adam could succeed.* He closed his mind to thoughts of his future, whispered a desperate prayer, and set out to enjoy this bright, God-given day.

After spending the morning together, they enjoyed lunch with the talkative Mrs. Gordon and the whole family. Then the children showed them their world, tumbling around them as they escorted them down to the river paddock to admire the new foal. When the children were at last called back to the house and their assorted chores, John and Elizabeth wandered hand in hand beside the quiet water that sparkled and flowed between the tall river gums.

Neither mentioned the threat that hung over John. Mr. Gordon had promised that no one would be able to set foot on the property without the guards he had posted seeing them, and they were too happy and content in each other's company to worry.

At his urging, Elizabeth told John more of her life. He asked her many questions about her father and how a convict could possibly become such a respected citizen in this vast country. She told him about her childhood growing up first on a small farm near the Hawkesbury River that had been granted to her father on completion of his sentence.

He could picture her excitement when her father at last achieved his dream of taking up a large tract of land in the newly opened, rich countryside. However, he had refused to bring his wife and small child with him. There was to be no camping rough under canvas for the woman who had lowered herself to marry him.

John thrilled at the gleam in her bright green eyes as Elizabeth laughed up at him and said, "But Mother had a mind of her own. She put up with not seeing him only for a few weeks. We were both so miserable without him, and one day we just packed up what we could and went to be with him. At first Father was angry, but Mother always told me that he was so happy to have us that he just finished building the bush hut as quickly as he could."

She was silent for awhile, and looking down at her shining hair, John knew just how lonely that man must have been without the woman he had loved and his beautiful daughter.

"But the sheep did very well, and it was only a few years before Father built us our lovely Waverley homestead," Elizabeth continued softly. "Oh, John, I do want you to see my home. It has not a large number of rooms, but it is so cozy and charming. I know it may not be as grand as you told me your mother's house was in Spain, or even Farnley Manor in Yorkshire, but it is made of special stone Father had hauled from the nearby hills. When the sun shines on it in a certain way, it sparkles and gleams as though it is alive. It was so good to see it again after all those years in England."

A cold shiver swept through John. Suddenly the peace of the day was shattered. She was a young lady who had been to a finishing school, had mixed with aristocrats. His life for the foreseeable future was to be on the wind-swept plains of Stevens Downs. There was no way he could ever ask her to leave her home for a rough, lonely hut, with Molly Hardy the only woman for hundreds of miles.

thirteen

Elizabeth took great delight in telling John all about her life before she had met him, including those years in England. She refrained from telling him about her Aunt Sophia's attempts at matchmaking, especially about the Honorable Frederick. But in the midst of her happiness, she suddenly realized John had gone quiet.

She paused and studied his face. His teeth flashed white as he smiled briefly at her, but his eyes were grave. A tremor passed through her, but she smiled blithely back at him and continued telling him about the very difficult last twelve months.

"Fortunately Adam trained a reliable man to take his place as chief stockman so he could leave the property with an easier mind while he struck out on his own. But there were still tough decisions to make." She hesitated and then said quietly, "The biggest one still has not been made. Some people have been urging me to sell out."

John's head swung toward her.

"Everyone, including the Richmonds, keep telling me it's too lonely a life for a young girl with no family, it's not suitable, fitting." She dared to glance up at John's thoughtful face. When she saw the slight frown on his face, she added hurriedly, "I told them I'm not really alone. There are good people in the bush. Everyone helps each other. And besides," she hesitated only slightly before adding firmly, "my heavenly Father is always with me wherever I am."

She smiled up at him and caught his dark glance. She saw him swallow and waited hopefully. Not once had he made any attempt to kiss her since that first moment in the barn. Yet she had been sure he had wanted to. Several times she had seen love for her darken his eyes, but each time he had turned sharply away.

Like he did now.

Perhaps she would have to take Mrs. Richmond's advice after all. Elizabeth scowled. It was all right listening and agreeing silently to Mrs. Richmond's idea about doing the proposing, but it was an entirely different thing plucking up the courage to be so forward!

"How long will it take to ride to your home?" John asked abruptly. "I think perhaps we should go there today after all."

Elizabeth stared up at him for a moment and then said in a flat voice, "Mrs. Gordon and the children will be disappointed."

"But we really should let Timothy and the others know I am all right. Besides, he must be anxious to reach Stevens Downs."

As much as Elizabeth desired to prolong this time with him, she had to agree. However, neither were prepared for the extent of their hostess's concern.

"Deary, deary me," Mrs. Gordon said with a worried frown, "Himself's been fetched by one of his men to help get one of them stupid cows out of a bog. He won't be at all happy about your going alone, and there's no man here to go with you."

John did hesitate at that, but Elizabeth said easily, "But my men are still here, aren't they?"

"Yes," she was told reluctantly, "but I know he intended to send more with you."

"Oh, I'm sure our Mr. Edwards has returned to Sydney by now. If not, he must be very uncomfortable by this time camping out," Elizabeth said with a smile.

By the time they had saddled up and departed, Elizabeth knew it would be nearly dark before they reached her home, but she said nothing, just set a quick pace over the paddocks. They would have made it before dark, too, if John's old horse had not put its foot in a hole. Fortunately he managed to keep his seat, but when they examined the limping horse, the verdict was it could not be ridden further.

"Oh, well, it's fortunate we are so close to home," Elizabeth said cheerfully. "Timothy's horse is certainly the strongest. You can double up behind me, and one of the men can lead your horse. It will mean a slow ride, though."

She saw John sway suddenly as he moved toward her. Biting her lip, she kept her horse steady as he heaved himself up behind her. But she heard his grunt of pain and knew that he must have pulled hard on his sore shoulder when his horse had stumbled.

"Look, it will be dark soon. You ride ahead to the house and bring back a sulky," she said to one of the men. "John will be able to hold his horse's reins."

The man she had spoken to hesitated and glanced around. They were in a clearing, but the shadows were darkening very rapidly.

"I'm feeling very tired," Elizabeth said more wearily than she really felt.

To her relief, John snapped, "You heard Miss Waverley. Perhaps you'd better both go. There's safety in numbers. Keep your eyes open, and if you see anything or anyone suspicious, come back immediately."

The men nodded. The horse's reins were passed to John. They kicked their horses into a canter and were gone.

Neither John nor Elizabeth spoke. John's hands around her waist tightened, and she felt as though she could travel for miles like this with him.

After some time she stirred and said contentedly, "Well, this is the last thick patch of scrub before the Home Paddock. They should be back soon with the sulky, and then we'll be home before—"

She broke off as they both heard a horse's soft snort and jingling bridle. John suddenly let go of his horse and put both arms around Elizabeth's waist. He dug his heels into the sides of the horse, but even as the horse leaped forward, it was too late.

The other horse loomed in front of them and blocked their

way. Light gleamed on the rifle held in Cecil Edwards' hand.

John saw it come up and yelled, "Look out!"

He felt Elizabeth jerk on the reins and gripped the horse tightly with his knees. The horse shied as the gun roared and a bullet whistled past their eyes.

"Hey, hey, you won't escape me this time," a crazy voice screamed at them.

Desperately John clung to Elizabeth as she hauled on the reins to turn her horse. He had already observed that she was a superb horsewoman, but the track was so narrow there was little room to maneuver.

He glanced back and saw the rifle come up again. Frantically he tried to shield her slender body with his own. Then another tall shadow slipped from the trees beside them, and he stared in despair. One they might have escaped, but two?

A harsh, grim voice roared, "You murderin' swine! So you'd even kill the lady, would you?"

A gun belched forth its fire. Cecil Edwards let out a scream of agony and toppled from his horse. Their horse reared violently at the noise so close to it. A strong arm flew out to grab the bridle and a strangely calm, but rough voice spoke soothing words until it again stood still.

Then they heard the sound of men shouting, and several horsemen galloped around the bend in the track from the direction of the house.

The tall, filthy man holding their horse gave a sharp curse and let go. He made a grab for Edwards' horse and in a flash was in the saddle. For a brief moment, he stared at Elizabeth and John.

Then in a soft voice he said, "It were for me mate, Jimmy. I bin a followin' 'im, you see, ma'am. He were a very bad man. I be glad 'e did you and yours no harm. You'll tell them it were for me mate."

Then he shook the horse's reins and was past them just as the first horseman arrived. It was Timothy, and then another voice behind him called out anxiously. A very unexpected voice.

"Elizabeth! Are you all right, my dear child?"

"Dr. Richmond?" she whispered shakily, and then she slipped from the horse and was clasping her guardian's hands in both of hers.

He peered into her face and then looked over her shoulder. "You are both all right? We heard the shots, and were afraid. . ."

Timothy shouted, "Dr. Richmond, sir! Edwards is hurt bad but still alive."

Elizabeth turned to John and buried her face in his strong shoulder. After a long moment when her trembling had eased, he put her gently aside and strode over to the men crouched around Cecil Edwards. Elizabeth followed him shakily.

As John knelt down, a weak, panting voice called out, "Martin? Did I get him for my old friend? Is he dead?"

John stared at him and then briefly across his body at Dr. Richmond. He saw him shake his head slightly and knew the man was dying.

"I'm still here, Edwards," he said sharply. "Your shot missed us."

Edwards stared up at him, while the dark stain spread deeper into the earth beneath him. "Like it did on the ship. Well, don't think you're safe. You'll never be safe while he. . .he's after you." He coughed once, and then his head fell back.

John crouched in a stupefied silence, his brain working furiously. *Someone else wanted him dead?*

It was Dr. Richmond who put his thought into a question. "Someone else is after Mr. Martin? Who is it, Edwards?"

The eyes were closed, and for a moment they thought he had gone. Then he opened them and said in a barely audible voice, "At first it was for Percy I made your life as miserable as I could. He. . .saved my life once you know. He. . .found out I was on your ship. . .asked me to. . .to. . .see you didn't make it. Then. . .then I hated you for my own sake. Because of you I've lost everything. . .everything. . ."

"No, Edwards, you've lost because of your own sinful nature," John said sternly. "Only God can save you now."

"God? Once I did think there was. . .God. . .but not. . .now. . ." The faltering voice stopped and the head fell back.

Dr. Richmond examined him for a moment, and then slowly stood up. Elizabeth gave a soft sob, and John sprang to his feet and led her away.

"Oh, how dreadful to die without God!" she sobbed quietly as he tried to comfort her.

John's brain was working furiously. Percy? Had he meant Percival Farnley, his father's heir? The man who had sat each day in that courtroom, who had seemed shaken at the transportation sentence? Had it been because he had hoped for the death penalty?

"What was it he said right at the end, John?" Elizabeth asked tearfully, and in that brief moment he made his decision.

"Just that he hated me, that once he had thought there was a God," he said softly. He must make sure Dr. Richmond did not tell her the rest. There was no point in worrying her now that the threat to them had gone. There was nothing more that Percival Farnley could do. He was fifteen hundred miles away across the ocean.

Later that evening after Elizabeth had at last gone to bed, John did have a chance to speak privately to Dr. Richmond. The moment they were alone, the older man fixed him with a piercing glance and asked, "Now, Mr. Martin, do you know who this Percy fellow is that wants to put a period to your life?"

John looked back at the doctor steadily and said, "The only man by that name I know of is my cousin Percival Farnley."

"Farnley?" The doctor frowned. "Is not that the name of the man you claim is your father?"

John knew Elizabeth had told the Richmonds his story, so he raised his chin and said firmly, "Lord Farnley is my father, but he has refused to acknowledge me. His heir is his brother's eldest child, Percival Farnley."

Dr. Richmond nodded slowly, not taking his eyes from John's face. "I do hope that Adam is extremely careful when he starts making enquiries for you in England," he said at long last.

John relaxed and smiled grimly. "Adam being the man he is, I know he will. We have already discussed my cousin and his role in the whole thing." He drew a deep breath. "Besides, I no longer care about Percival or the Farnleys. If Adam's investigations are successful, so be it, if not. . ." He shrugged.

He hesitated only briefly and then raised his chin and looked at Dr. Richmond steadily. "You may not choose to believe me, sir, but these last few days I have realized as never before that I am in a loving God's hands. He has promised me His joy, no matter what man does to me, whether I am John Martin or Lord Farnley, whether I am convict or free man, whether. . ."

His voice cracked, but his steady gaze did not waver. "Sir, I. . .I want to assure you that your ward is safe from my attentions."

To his surprise the doctor gave a sudden bark of a laugh and rolled his eyes heavenward. "My dear sir, you can be assured you are not safe from Elizabeth Waverley's attentions!" He gave a helpless shrug. "She will be her own mistress in a few months, but for what it is worth, you do have my permission to pay your addresses to her. As a point of fact, you no longer even need permission from the authorities to marry."

Suddenly John could not move.

Dr. Richmond pulled out a couple sheets of paper from his coat pocket and thrust them at John. "For the past year I have felt exceedingly guilty at my part in separating our dear Elizabeth from you. For months now I have been petitioning the powers that be on your behalf, bombarding them with Adam Stevens' glowing reports of your exemplary conduct. They decided at last that after twelve months you did need some more recompense for what happened aboard the *Royal Lady*, as well as the cowardly attack on your person the other night."

He gave a very ungentlemanly snort. "Perhaps they also realized I was not going to stop asking, or perhaps with all the current turmoil about self-government and the abolition of transportation they did not want your story to reach our fledgling newspapers. For whatever reason, they at last granted my requests, even to rushing things through so I could try and catch up with you."

He shook the papers impatiently at John. "Here, take them. I can assure you they will be of great interest to you."

John glanced blindly down, and his hands closed around the papers.

Before he could speak, the doctor added wearily, "Now, I am too tired for more talk. I had not long arrived here when the word came that made us go out to escort you home. We have ridden hard, with only the hard ground to sleep on for a few hours last night."

John opened his mouth, but Dr. Richmond said testily, "Good night, Mr. Martin. We shall speak again in the morning." Then he bowed and walked out.

John stared after him in a daze and then down at the papers in his hand. *He did not need permission to marry?* That could only mean one thing. *Was it possible? Was this more evidence of God's goodness and care?*

Then he looked around at the luxurious room, and his heart sank. How could he possibly ask a woman like Elizabeth to give up all this and marry him?

He slowly spread open the documents and started to read.

ॐ

Elizabeth woke early. The morning sun streamed into her room and across her face. Memories of the previous day rushed into her mind. Before going to sleep, she had let the tears soak into her pillow for a life that been so wasted.

Now the sunshine dispelled the shadows of the night. The danger to John was gone. He would be safely assigned to Adam.

Instead of calling for her maid, she dressed quickly and went out into the garden. Although it was still early, the dew had already dried on the flowers. She paused beside the rose bushes her mother had planted so carefully many years ago. The summer roses were in full bloom, and she bent and caressed a velvety dark red petal.

"They are very beautiful, like their mistress," a deep voice said behind her.

She whirled around. "Oh, John, is it not a splendid morning? Are you an early riser too?"

He nodded briefly, and she noted that he looked even better than he had last night after he had washed and changed into his clean clothes, but he stared at her as though he had never seen her before. She frowned slightly at the tense, strained look on his face and then smiled at him. "I am glad you and Timothy have decided to stay a couple more days. It will give me a chance to show you some of Waverley and to pack my things."

His head jerked up. "Pack your things?"

She beamed innocently up at him, clenched her hands tightly behind her back, and said firmly, "Did not Timothy tell you? I'm coming with you all. I'm dying to see Stevens Downs," she continued chattily, turning to stroll over to another rose bush and pulling off a dead bud.

"Elizabeth, I. . ."

She carefully planted another smile on her face and turned toward him again, hoping that her trembling hands were not obvious to him.

He fixed her with a piercing glance. "Elizabeth, it is a very harsh place farther west." He looked around at the garden. "There is nothing like this. The dwellings are very basic, made from roughly hewn logs and bark with the insides lined in hessian and paper."

"Oh? I thought it would be like that," she said brightly. "It will remind me of our first house here when I was a child."

He did not move a muscle. She stared into his eyes and then moved toward him, hoping her legs would hold her up.

"There is something I have been meaning to ask you, John."

He still did not move as she came right up to him. Then she

saw his eyes were deep, dark pools of excitement and. . .and something else.

Her heart leaped. Perhaps she may not have to take Mrs. Richmond's advice after all.

A little breathlessly she said, "Is there any chance they could manage without you at Stevens Downs? I am very much in need of a trustworthy man to manage Waverley Station for me, and I wondered if I could have you assigned here to me."

A muscle in his tense jaw twitched. "I'm afraid that is not possible."

Elizabeth's courage was starting to fade rapidly under that relentless gaze. "What. . .what do you mean?" she faltered. "Don't you want to be here with me?"

Suddenly he reached for her, and she was folded so tightly against him she could hardly breathe. She raised her head, and his lips claimed hers again and again until her senses went spinning off into space.

"Elizabeth!" he groaned at last. "I love you so desperately."

She was beyond words and put up a badly shaking hand and caressed his dark cheek. He turned his head and his lips kissed her palm fervently.

"You can't have me assigned to you, because last night. . ." The wonder and awe of it was in his voice, in his blazing eyes as he paused and then continued in a choked voice, "Last night Dr. Richmond gave me my ticket-of-leave papers."

She gave a joyful exclamation and hugged him tighter still. "Oh, John, I'm so pleased for you! That means you can live wherever you want to in New South Wales, work wherever you want to."

He returned her embrace fervently, but at last he said with a trace of sadness, "I can stay here or work for Adam if he still wants me. But he has been very good to me and is relying on me while he is away, so I must stay at Stevens Downs. Otherwise I could most certainly stay here with you."

"No wonder Mrs. Richmond was so excited! Did Dr. Richmond tell you how he managed to get it for you?"

"No, he just gave it to me with. . .with another piece of paper last night." The strained note was back in his beloved voice. He suddenly let his hands drop away from her and took a step back. He looked so serious that she stared up at him anxiously.

"Elizabeth, you do realize that even with a ticket-of-leave I could remain a convict for a long time, perhaps forever, don't you?"

She was silent. *Was he about to say good-bye?*

Fear swept through her. She offered up a fervent, silent prayer. Instantly God's love swept her fear away.

She tilted her head and said steadily, "Our God is faithful, John. He has been with us both through so much. He could have you proved innocent, or failing that, even a pardon from the governor. Or perhaps He would have you just stay as a convict. It is all in His control. It doesn't really matter. I love you," she finished simply.

He closed his eyes for a moment, swallowed, and then looked at her with so much love and tenderness in his eyes that she could not breathe.

"Then, would you do me the honor of marrying that convict, Miss Waverley?"

His voice cracked on her name. It brought her out of her stupor into vibrant, pulsating life.

"Oh, yes! Please yes! It is what I have longed for above all else!"

Then he kissed her again.

This time it was a reverent, awe-inspiring embrace, as a man and a woman would kiss before the loving eyes of their heavenly Father. God's love and peace enveloped them both. It was He and He alone who had kept them, had worked out all things, and would continue to work all things out for good for the rest of their lives.

A Letter To Our Readers

Dear Reader:

In order that we might better contribute to your reading enjoyment, we would appreciate your taking a few minutes to respond to the following questions. We welcome your comments and read each form and letter we receive. When completed, please return to the following:

Rebecca Germany, Fiction Editor
Heartsong Presents
PO Box 719
Uhrichsville, Ohio 44683

1. Did you enjoy reading *Faith in the Great Southland?*
   ❑ Very much. I would like to see more books
      by this author!
   ❑ Moderately
      I would have enjoyed it more if _____
      _____
      _____

2. Are you a member of **Heartsong Presents**? Yes ❑ No ❑
   If no, where did you purchase this book? _____
   _____

3. How would you rate, on a scale from 1 (poor) to 5 (superior),
   the cover design? _____

4. On a scale from 1 (poor) to 10 (superior), please rate the
   following elements.

   _____ Heroine   _____ Plot

   _____ Hero   _____ Inspirational theme

   _____ Setting   _____ Secondary characters

5. These characters were special because _____

    _____

    _____

6. How has this book inspired your life? _____

    _____

    _____

7. What settings would you like to see covered in future
    Heartsong Presents books? _____

    _____

    _____

8. What are some inspirational themes you would like to see
    treated in future books? _____

    _____

    _____

9. Would you be interested in reading other **Heartsong
    Presents** titles?   Yes ❑   No ❑

10. Please check your age range:
    ❑ Under 18   ❑ 18-24   ❑ 25-34
    ❑ 35-45   ❑ 46-55   ❑ Over 55

11. How many hours per week do you read? _____

Name _____

Occupation _____

Address _____

City _____ State _____ Zip _____

Ah, those homemade,

comforting family dinners around the table. But who has time to make them between carpooling and softball games?

Don't let your busy schedule deter you. This collection of delectable recipes—from the readers and authors of inspirational romances—has been gathered from all over the United States, and even from Greece and Australia.

There are tried and true recipes for every occasion—Crock-Pot meals for busy days, fast desserts for church dinners, rave snacks for after school, holiday gifts for those picky relatives, and much, much more. Over 700 recipes await you! Bring back the joy of treasured moments over good food with the ones you love. So, dust off the china and treat your loved ones (and yourself) to some delicious home cooking.

The Heart's Delight *cookbook has what every family needs—cooking from the heart.*

400 pages, Paperbound, 8" x 5 ³/₁₆"

Please send me _____ copies of *Heart's Delight*. I am enclosing $4.97 each. (Please add $1.00 to cover postage and handling per order. OH add 6% tax.)

Send check or money order, no cash or C.O.D.s please.

Name_____

Address _____

City, State, Zip _____

To place a credit card order, call 1-800-847-8270.
Send to: Heartsong Presents Reader Service
PO Box 719, Uhrichsville, OH 44683

·····Hearts♥ng·····

HEARTSONG PRESENTS TITLES AVAILABLE NOW: